'There's a lot
don't know, Pr

She caught a glimpse .... coming down
across his features before he turned sharply on his
heel and walked over to the first patient's bed. The
game had begun.

During the entire ward round his mood remained
black and he was determined to punish Penny for
it. Penny, however, was in the mood to retaliate
and accepted his challenge without batting an
eyelid.

Lucy Clark began writing romance in her early teens and immediately knew she'd found her 'calling' in life. After working as a secretary in a busy teaching hospital, she turned her hand to writing medical romances. She currently lives in Adelaide, Australia, and has the desire to travel the world with her husband. Lucy largely credits her writing success to the support of her husband, family and friends.

A SURGEON'S CARE

BY
LUCY CLARK

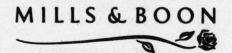

MILLS & BOON

Many thanks to the SA Romance Writers' Group, Tony, Siobhan, my family—especially Glenda and Pete. I couldn't have done it without your love, support and help.
Psalm 37:4

MILLS & BOON, the Rose Device and
LOVE ON CALL are trademarks of the publisher.
Harlequin Mills & Boon Limited,
Eton House, 18-24 Paradise Road, Richmond, Surrey TW9 1SR

© Lucy Clark 1996

ISBN 0 263 79859 3

Set in Times 10 on 11 pt. by
Rowland Phototypesetting Limited
Bury St Edmunds, Suffolk

03-9611-48420

Made and printed in Great Britain

CHAPTER ONE

'WHEW! I'm beat. What a list!' Theatre Sister remarked to Penny. 'I don't know how you do it.'

'You'll get used to it in time,' Penny laughed, shaking her short brown curls free from her surgical cap. She had been operating in the emergency theatres all morning. 'How long have you been in Adelaide?'

'This is my third week. I've just come from a small country hospital in New Zealand,' Sister groaned, sitting on a chair and rubbing her feet.

Any further conversation the two women might have had was interrupted by the sound of Penny's pager. She looked reluctantly at the number.

'It's General Theatre,' she moaned.

'They must really need you. Twice in Theatre and again now! That's three times in the last twenty minutes.'

'It's because the new department head is starting today. I guess they want everything to be as efficient as possible.'

Saying a hurried goodbye to the sister, Penny raced up the stairs to General Theatre. She felt nervous about meeting Professor Samuel Chadwick as his reputation had preceded him, even to the extent that his previous hospital had sent a sympathy card to the orthopaedic staff.

She quickly scrubbed and donned the necessary theatre garments and as she entered a sniffling theatre nurse passed her on the way out. Oh, dear! Was he as bad as all that?

The operation was a routine one but it would be interesting to see the famous Professor Chadwick perform it. Open reduction and internal fixation of a fractured tibia simplistically meant that he would cut where the bone was broken and fit the pieces together before securing them with a metal plate and screws.

As she approached the operating table her brown eyes encountered eyes of icy blue. The ice thawed a little, momentarily, as they stared deep into her soul. He looked back to his work, the contact broken.

'Where on earth is Dr Hatfield?' he demanded of the theatre sister. He didn't raise his voice but it held a strong note of impatience.

Penny cleared her throat. 'Where do you want me, Professor Chadwick?'

The moment the words were out of her mouth Penny regretted them. What had made her voice so husky? Blue eyes snapped up to look at her again, raking over her theatre gown and up-held hands. It was a few seconds before he replied and Penny found herself holding her breath.

'Well, I can certainly think up quite a few answers to that question, Dr Hatfield.' His voice had softened and she could tell by his twinkling eyes that he was laughing at her. 'But for the moment could you hold this retractor?'

Penny blushed beneath her mask, glad of its shield. What a perfect voice. It was as smooth as silk. Between his eyes and his voice Professor Chadwick was having a devastating effect on her equilibrium. What would happen when he de-gowned and she saw the rest of him?

She risked a glance at him but found him absorbed in his work. A wave of guilt swept over her. She, too, should be absorbed in her work, not day-dreaming about her new boss.

They finished the theatre list on time and Penny was thankful that her day was almost over. A quick ward round and then she was free. She changed out of her theatre blues into khaki shorts and a white shirt. These mid-February afternoons were still very hot.

Walking out of the ward after seeing her patients, Penny literally collided with Derek, her fellow registrar.

'Hey, Penny. Had a tough day in Theatre?' He stood with his hands in his dark brown trouser pockets, stethoscope hung round his neck, and striped shirt unbuttoned at the top to reveal a smooth chest.

'Yes, as a matter of fact I did.' She massaged one hand along the back of her neck and grinned at her colleague. 'Does your presence here mean that you are now officially back from leave?'

'I guess it does,' he smiled back. Derek's smile, coupled with his blue eyes and fair hair, had melted many a heart. Fortunately Penny was immune to his charms and they had been good friends for the past ten years. They'd dated for a short time in their first year of medical school but had soon realised that there was no spark between them. 'Say, have you met the new Prof yet?'

At the mention of the professor Penny felt something stir through her body.

'I was in Theatre with him this afternoon. It was a routine list but it was fantastic to work with him. He really is a magnificent surgeon,' she babbled.

Over the years she had been able to talk to Derek about anything but the feelings that Professor Chadwick stirred in her were not only ones of admiration and respect but also a tingling of anticipation.

These feelings she was determined to keep to herself until she had time to dissect them thoroughly.

Eager to escape Derek's intense gaze, she excused herself, saying she would see him tomorrow. She had some shopping to do in town and began the short walk to the mall.

After an hour of trying to find a suitable present for her brother's birthday and not having any success, Penny walked toward her favourite coffee-shop. Stretching out a hand to push the door open, she felt a hard masculine chest with a smooth cotton covering. Immediately mumbling an apology, she looked up into the smiling blue eyes of Professor Chadwick. She felt her entire body flood with colour but found it difficult to break eye contact. He was holding the door open for her but her feet were glued to the spot.

'Dr Hatfield. What a surprise.' He didn't sound surprised at all but the deep huskiness of his voice made her body tingle. She tried to open her mouth to say something but the words were lodged in her throat. Her eyes, making the most of their first opportunity to assess him without the bulk of his theatre garb, began to rove over his lean, taut body.

He was dressed casually in jeans and a blue cotton shirt the exact colour of his eyes. Penny's gaze raked him from head to toe a few more times before finally resting on his mouth. He was absolutely the most handsome man she had ever met! His perfect voice had a perfect body to match. She felt herself begin to sweat and the blush rose further when he laughed out loud.

'Do I measure up?' he drawled laconically.

'Oh, Professor Chadwick,' she managed on a whisper. 'I'm so sorry.'

'No, you're not. Anyway, I must admit I quite enjoyed it.' He took her elbow and ushered her inside to a secluded table for two. 'Let me buy you a coffee.'

She cleared her throat and began to find her confidence again. 'That's not necessary, Professor. You were on your way out so you obviously have another appointment.'

'Are you scared of me, Dr Hatfield?' he asked, his blue eyes twinkling mischievously.

Penny sat up straight in her chair, trying to control the irritation caused by her own stupidity at letting him get under her skin. 'Certainly not,' she stated hotly.

'Then why object to me buying you a coffee?'

Penny opened her mouth and then closed it again. How could she tell him that she had been pre-warned about his beastly personality? He was a fabulous surgeon but as for communication with his staff they did what he ordered or nothing at all. Registrars, interns and nursing staff had all been reduced to sniffling idiots from his fierce demands for perfection. She, herself, had seen evidence of this when she had walked into Theatre this afternoon.

'The matter is settled, then,' he stated firmly when she failed to reply and ordered her a cappuccino. 'You look rather tired, Dr Hatfield. Busier day than usual?'

'No, not really. For the past hour I've been shopping for a present for my brother's birthday.'

'What did you end up buying?' he asked, a quizzical smile on his lips.

'Nothing. I couldn't find a darned thing I thought he'd like. I thought it better to sit down and think a bit more before I start shopping again.' She paused for breath and then continued apologetically, 'I'm sorry, Professor. I didn't mean to babble on like that.'

He held up a hand. 'No need to apologise. In fact, I'm quite pleased that I. . .er. . .bumped into you.'

'Why?' A frown creased her forehead.

'Because I wanted a chance to get to know you better,' he answered simply.

Penny felt her heart execute several somersaults. He wanted to know about her? Why? No! He must just want to talk about the hospital. Yes, that's all, she told herself, and berated her heart for behaving like a love-sick teenager. She made certain that she had control over her voice before she spoke.

'Sure, Professor. What is it about the hospital that you'd like to know?'

Samuel Chadwick leaned forward in his chair, resting his elbows on the table and his chin on his hands. 'First of all, I'd like to know how I can get you to stop calling me ''Professor''. And, secondly, I want to know everything there is to know about Penny Hatfield. The person, not the doctor.'

Her eyes widened in disbelief and her voice was a whisper. 'But Profess. . .'

'My name is Sam,' he said, reaching out to cup his hand over hers. 'There is no work, no hospital, no operating, no rules, no ethics. There is just you and I, Penny.'

Looking into his baby-blue eyes, Penny could see that he was intent on doing exactly as he had said. Why he should choose to get to know her better was beyond her means of rational thought. The effect he was having on her equilibrium was bewildering and she was positive that if he didn't break the contact with her hand soon then he and the whole coffee-shop would hear the wild, erratic beat of her heart.

'Just as well I'm sitting down, otherwise I might have fallen down,' she thought and then blushed as she realised she had spoken aloud. Sam chuckled and gave her hand a little squeeze. His eyes said that he understood her confusion and she was almost tempted to ask him to explain it to *her*.

'Well. . . Sam.' She tried his name on for size and found that it was a perfect fit on her lips. 'What do you want to know?'

'Everything!' The deep resonance of his voice vibrated through her fingertips, up her arm then exploded through her entire body.

Penny took a deep breath and began, 'I'm twenty-nine and am in my third year of advanced training, which means I'll be sitting my final exams next year. I grew up in Melbourne but moved to Adelaide when I started medical school. I decided to become an orthopod when I broke my femur in my third year of medical school. I love to go to the movies, dancing and I love Chinese food.' She grinned at him like a Cheshire cat. What more could the man want than that?

'Thank you, Penelope,' he said drily, releasing her hand and sitting back in his chair as the waiter brought their drinks. 'If I'd wanted particulars like that I could have read your résumé.'

'Well, why didn't you?' she questioned crossly. What was she supposed to tell him? She hardly knew the man. Maybe that was the problem, she analysed. The person sitting opposite her was exactly that. A man. Not Professor Samuel Chadwick, clinical director of the orthopaedic department. He had been kind, gentle and considerate to her since she had bumped into him and, to tell the truth, she liked the man that was being revealed.

So why not tell him a bit about yourself? her heart was telling her brain. This might be your one and only chance.

She spooned one sugar into her cappuccino and began to stir slowly. She glanced up at him, only to find that he was watching her every move. Her whole body suffused with heat and she swallowed hard over the dryness in her throat.

'I like to be wined, dined and romanced,' she said softly, coyly raising her eyes to meet his. He didn't move a muscle but his eyes held hers intently.

'I don't like a man to bring me just a bunch of flowers—I want a man to bring me my favourite flower. That way I know he's taken enough interest to find out what that is.' She used her spoon to scoop up a bit of froth from her cappuccino and slowly raised the spoon to her lips.

Sam nervously cleared his throat and once again rested his elbows on the table and his chin on his hands, giving her his undivided attention.

Penny dropped her voice to a seductive whisper. 'I need a man who is honest in every way. One who truly cares about me and respects my career. But most of all. . .' She trailed off and again raised a spoon full of froth to her lips. She quietly slurped the froth off the spoon, gave it a lick and replaced in on her saucer. Penny watched as Sam's Adam's apple began working up and down as he convulsively swallowed, his eyes intent on the movement of her lips.

'Most of all, when I'm alone with a man. . .' She sat lazily back in her chair and raised one eyebrow. The expression on Sam's face was one of unexpected delight and anxiousness. 'I like to beat him at Space Invaders on my computer,' she finished in a normal voice, completely breaking the seductive mood she had purposely set. The grin she gave him was a sassy one as she picked up her cappuccino and took a sip.

He cleared his throat again and returned her grin. 'Well, then. I'll have to make sure I practise on Space Invaders so that I can't be beaten.' He followed suit and began to drink his coffee. 'That way you'll have to play me until you win.' Now it was his turn to look sassy as Penny choked on her mouthful at his double meaning. At least he had a sense of humour.

'Take it easy there, Pen.' His shortened version of her name made her eyes dart up to him. Only her father called her that—no one else. But when Sam said it, it was more like a caress. A caress she found she liked— very much.

She glanced at her watch and let out a mortified yelp. 'Oh, no. The shops will be closing soon and I still haven't picked anything out for Eric.' She reached for her bag and began to stand. 'Thanks for the coffee, Sam, but I really do have to go.' She marvelled at the way his first name came so freely to her lips.

'Wait.' He rose, quickly dealt with the bill and took her elbow to usher her out of the shop. 'Mind if I tag along? I might be more of a help than a hindrance. After all I am a male,' he added, when she was about to refuse.

She looked him up and down. Yes, he was definitely male!

'OK,' she agreed. 'If you were turning sixteen and were crazy about cars, what would you want for your birthday?'

Sam frowned at her question, although she wasn't sure why. 'Eric's thirteen years younger than you?'

'Yeah. Mum and Dad's miracle baby. After she'd had me she suffered very bad endometriosis and was told she could have no more children.' They began to walk toward the shops.

'You didn't object to losing your status as one and only?'

'No. Quite the opposite. I'd always wanted a brother or sister. Eric is a darling and we get on very well.'

'When's his birthday?'

'Saturday. I was going to go shopping last weekend but we had a very big mop-up list and by the time I got out, well, you know the story.'

'All too well, I'm afraid,' he muttered. Sam steered Penny to a small hobby shop and there she was able to purchase the most appropriate present for her brother. A hand-made miniature replica of a Silver Ghost. She was sure that Eric would love it as he had spent hours at the motor museum looking at that very car. With that done, they made their way back to the hospital car park.

Expecting Sam to leave her at the entrance to the car parking station, Penny was pleasantly surprised when he announced that he would accompany her up the stairs to her car. She had thoroughly enjoyed the afternoon and was reluctant for it to end.

'Thank you very much for rescuing me from my dilemma, Sam,' Penny said after placing her package and bag in the car.

'The pleasure was all mine.' He smiled a heart-stopping smile at her and she unconsciously reached out a hand to the car for support. The air became charged with electricity as neither of them spoke for a few moments.

'Well.' Penny cleared her throat. 'I'll see you tomorrow.'

'Sure.' He stepped forward and lightly brushed his lips across hers before turning toward the stairwell.

How she managed to get home was a miracle as far as Penny was concerned. Arriving at the small unit she lived in by herself, she was surprised to realise that she had no recollection of the short drive home from the hospital. At least she hadn't had to make the hour-long

journey to her parents' home south of Adelaide. It was
a wonderful retreat when she wasn't on call but she
doubted whether she could have made it on autopilot.

She sorted through her mail and began to thaw some
food for her meal. Her body was still tingling with
delight at Sam's kiss. She knew it would be foolhardy
to read too much into one brief kiss but she couldn't
help herself. At least for tonight she would have the
right to dream of Samuel Chadwick.

She watched an old Cary Grant movie on television,
all the time imagining that Sam was Cary Grant and
she his leading lady.

At the end of the movie she switched off the box
with a nostalgic sigh and started getting ready for bed.

'Whadizzit?' she asked as someone shook her shoulder,
waking her from a very dreary sleep. Slumped over a
desk in the registrar's office with her head buried on
her arms, she was as comfortable as if she were sleeping
on a cloud.

She had been woken at five o'clock that morning
with an emergency. Derek had been first on take but
the night had been a busy one and they'd needed her
at the hospital as well.

Her patient's name was Maureen Brooker. She had
fallen down the stairs inside her house and had fractured her right arm and leg in several places. Mrs
Brooker had been unconscious for at least half an hour
after the fall before she'd managed to crawl her way
to the telephone and ring for help.

She was also heavily bruised, which had bothered
Penny at the time. Bruising would occur naturally but
these bruises were everywhere and Penny was determined to question Mrs Brooker as soon as possible.

It was now two o'clock in the afternoon and Penny

had only escaped from Theatre half an hour ago. She wouldn't be this tired if she had managed to stop thinking about Samuel Chadwick. But she had lain awake until at least four a.m., only to be woken an hour later.

'I told you to wake me at two o'clock. It's only been five minutes. Leave me alone,' she mumbled incoherently to the ward sister who she'd told to wake her.

The hand on her shoulder shook her again but the voice that spoke was masculine.

'Come on, Penny, rise and shine. It's patient time,' Derek's chirpy voice rang out.

'Yeah, sure,' she grumbled, raising her head and looking at him through bleary eyes. 'You've been home. Managed to catch a few extra hours' sleep, leaving me with the really hard cases.' She let out a growl as Derek beamed down at her.

'Yep.' Swine—he didn't sound repentant at all. 'Hang in there, Penny. Only five more days until your holidays.' He gently began to massage her shoulders and she groaned with relief.

'Mmm.' She closed her eyes. 'That feels nice, Derek.' Suddenly his hands stopped and fell away from her. She turned and looked up at him then followed his gaze to the door. Sam was standing there, impeccably dressed in dark navy trousers, crisp white shirt and silk tie. He wore a white coat over the top of his shirt, stethoscope strategically placed around his neck.

He looked gorgeous and Penny could feel her body begin to respond again. It was the first time she had seen him since he'd left her at the car park yesterday. Why did that seem so long ago?

'OK, Chalmers.' He spoke to Derek, his voice as sharp and as cool as ice. 'Get to Clinic. Hatfield, get out of those theatre blues and get your butt up to Clinic as soon as possible.'

Sam moved out of the way as Derek rushed through the door but barred it again as Penny rose to her feet and glared back at him.

'Is there a problem, Sam?' she queried calmly as she walked toward him.

'Please address me as Professor and I will not tolerate any members of my staff slacking off while they are still on duty.'

Penny opened her mouth to protest but he held up a hand to silence her.

'We all work long hours; we all have to cope with delays, hold-ups, busy clinics. You are no exception, Dr Hatfield,' he stated firmly, his eyes now a steely, cold blue.

'I never asked to be.' She finally overcame her shock enough to say something.

'I would also like to point out that I do not appreciate my staff openly flirting in the registrar's office in full view of the entire world.'

'But. . .' she stammered, then realised that it was futile to reason with him in this mood. Here was his temper, fully blown. The professor at his best.

'Don't argue, Hatfield. Now go and change. I'll expect you in Clinic in five minutes. No more.' He turned sharply on his heel and stalked off down the corridor.

'Yes, Professor,' she spat at his retreating back. Where was the man I met yesterday? her heart asked. Obviously he's disappeared and his awful twin brother has taken his place, her head answered.

CHAPTER TWO

'OK, MRS GREGORY.' Penny stood in front of her patient. 'I'd like to see you again in two weeks' time. I'll order another X-ray, just to double-check that the fracture is in a good position and then the plaster should be able to come off four weeks after that. If you have any problems in the meantime just ring the hospital and have me paged.' She smiled at the elderly woman before turning to fill in the case notes.

'Could you see one more patient before you finish, Dr Hatfield?' Sister Williamson walked into the room and, relieving Penny of Mrs Gregory's notes, handed her a new file. 'Mr Mark Shields, a nineteen-year-old man who races go-karts. He has a very painful right knee which he injured at age fifteen but it didn't require surgical intervention. He reported to Casualty half an hour ago. They took one look at him and sent him up here. The Prof insisted that you see him so I've put him in clinic room three.'

Penny sighed heavily. What had she done to deserve Sam's wrath?

'I'm sorry, Penny,' Sister Williamson said softly. 'I tried to pass it on to someone else because I know you've been up half the night but he insisted.'

'It's all right, Lauren. We might as well get it over and done with.' Penny took the file and went into clinic room three.

'Mr Shields, I'm Dr Hatfield. I believe you've done something to your right knee. Can you tell me exactly what happened?'

18

'Hey. I ain't seeing no lady doctor,' Mark Shields sneered through rotten teeth. Penny stopped for a moment and just looked at her patient. Every visible inch of him was tattooed and Penny was sure that he had tattoos in the places that weren't visible as well. He had a beer gut, a shaggy beard and long black hair. 'Where'd you get your licence from? A cereal packet?' Mark Shields tried to climb off the examination couch but was met with strong resistance from his right leg. Penny and Lauren exchanged a glance over the top of his bent head.

'Ow!' he wailed. 'I'm in so much pain. Just give me somethin' for the pain and then I'll wait and see a real doctor,' he howled and Penny was certain that everyone else in the clinic had heard him.

'I need some more details from you, Mr Shields. How exactly did you injure your knee?'

'I ain't tell you nothin'. No woman is going to treat me.'

Penny was exhausted and in no mood to play games with nineteen-year-old babies. She bent to look at his knee but didn't touch it. Mark tried to kick her but only ended up with more excruciating pain surging up his leg.

'That was foolish.' Penny straightened and motioned to Lauren. 'Please have an orderly take Mr Shields to X-Ray.' Penny scribbled her instructions on an X-ray form and handed it to Lauren.

Penny could see beads of sweat breaking out over Mark's forehead. The pain must be increasing and he could do with a little calming down. She reviewed his notes and the case history that had been taken. As far as this hospital knew, he wasn't allergic to any drugs. He'd received analgesics in Casualty in the form of Panadeine but that was all.

'Mr Shields, as far as you know are you allergic to any drugs? Penicillin, pethidine, Valium, that sort of thing?'

'No.' The answer was given through clenched teeth.

'Have you taken anything for the pain? Paracetamol, Panadeine?'

'Two measly little tablets from downstairs.' Again through clenched teeth.

Penny administered one hundred milligrams of pethidine. 'Mr Shields, an orderly will come with a wheelchair and take you down to the X-ray department. Once you've finished there I'll review your X-rays and your knee.'

On her way out of the clinic room she almost collided with the professor.

'Sorry, Prof.' She stepped back to let him pass but not before she noticed a frown crease his forehead.

'What's going on in there?' he growled and her eyes widened in surprise at his tone. What was his problem?

'Just a mild case of chauvinism. I've handled worse.' Penny neatly sidestepped his frame and began walking down the short corridor. She needed coffee and fast.

She was sitting in the cafeteria drinking her second cup of coffee when she was paged. That would mean that her darling patient was back and ready for her to examine. She wondered, as she walked back to the clinic, whether she should put on some protective clothing before she examined Mr Shields. Something in the way of a suit of armour.

She was chuckling to herself when she entered the clinic room. Mark Shields glared at her with all the chauvinistic contempt he could muster.

'Now, Mr Shields,' Penny smiled. That coffee had made all the difference. 'I see the X-ray department has sent you back to me still in one piece. Let's have a look at the films they've so kindly taken and see if we can fix you up.'

'I told you before. I ain't gonna let no lady doctor near me.'

'How are you today, Mr Shields?' Sam walked into the room and Penny turned to glare at him. What did he think he was doing?

'Finally, a real doctor to fix me up,' Mark said with relief.

'I believe Dr Hatfield was just about to do that. Continue, Dr Hatfield.' Sam stood with his arms folded across his chest in the direct vision of Mr Shields. Mark just sat there as good as gold as Penny examined his knee.

As Lauren attended to their patient Penny motioned for Sam to follow her so that they could look at the X-rays. Usually this was done at the viewing box in every clinic room but Penny didn't want Mark to cause any more trouble and, besides, she wanted an opportunity to have a word or two with Sam.

'How dare you come in and interfere with my patient?' she exploded as soon as they were safe in a clinic room across the corridor.

'I didn't interfere. In fact, I just stood there. You needed help and as he's the last patient and everyone else has gone home I thought I'd give you a hand.'

'I've handled his kind before, Sam, and I was doing fine.'

'Well, there's no point in arguing about it now. What do the X-rays show?'

'He's fractured the kneecap—' Penny hooked the X-rays onto the viewing box '—and chipped the thigh bone joint surface. I'll operate tomorrow morning after he's fasted. An open reduction with tension band wiring of the kneecap. I'll carefully examine the thigh bone joint surface to check if there is a fracture involving the bony surface as well,' Penny explained sarcastically, still angry with Sam, then turned on her heel and went back to her patient.

'Mr Shields.' He was now quietly lying on the examination couch, almost snoozing. 'You'll need to be admitted to hospital tonight and will be operated on tomorrow morning. Who brought you here, Mr Shields?'

'My mate, Steve. He's still waiting for me.'

'Is there anyone else we can contact? Your parents?'

'Don't have any. Steve can get whatever I need.'

Penny left the clinic room to go and fetch Steve, who was a long-haired, long-bearded man in his mid-twenties. He, too, was heavily tattooed but had a slightly worried look on his face.

'Steve?' Penny held out her hand. The man stood, his height well over six feet. 'I'm Dr Hatfield. I'll be taking care of Mr Shields.'

Steve's whole body began to shake convulsively. 'Mark got stuck with a sheila. Serves him right.' Steve laughed and Penny crossed her arms defensively. 'Nothing personal, Doc. Just that Mark's a real chauvinistic pig.'

'So I'd noticed,' Penny muttered to herself. 'Well, I'm afraid that Mr Shields needs to have his knee operated on. I'll be taking him to Theatre tomorrow morning and he will be admitted to the ward immediately. He will be needing a few necessities for his stay and, as I understand it, he would like you to collect these things for him. If you'll follow the orderly down to the ward with Mr Shields you can discuss what he needs then. Do you have any questions?'

*   *   *

Penny was glad to leave the clinic and was even happier when she walked to the car park after admitting Mark Shields. She'd been at that wretched hospital for almost fourteen hours and had been on her feet for most of it.

'Penny.'

She turned to find Sam striding toward her. That was all she needed. Another argument with Sam when she was dead dog tired.

'Fancy something to eat?' Sam smiled down at her but Penny was too exhausted to be bowled over by his smile this time.

'Yes, I do, and I'm going home on my own to get it.' She turned and continued walking to the car park.

'I meant did you want to have dinner together.' He walked beside her.

'I know what you meant, Sam. I chose to misinterpret it.' She stopped when she reached the car parking station stairwell. 'I'm just too tired for company, Sam. I want to go home and relax, then go to sleep. I've had an awful day and the sooner it ends the better.'

'Let me buy dinner and we'll eat it at your place. That way you don't have to cook or do dishes and you can sleep as soon as you like,' he offered.

'I don't understand you, Samuel Chadwick. First you're nice to me then you're mean and now you want to be nice again. I just don't get it.'

'It's called separating your personal and professional lives,' Sam replied. 'After working hours I'm plain old Sam Chadwick but during hours I'm the professor.'

'Split personality or maybe you're twins. One nice, one awful.' Penny shook her head and started climbing the stairs.

'I'll be around in twenty minutes with dinner,' Sam yelled up the stairwell but Penny ignored him.

*　　*　　*

Sam was true to his word and turned up on her doorstep with Chinese take-away precisely twenty minutes from when they had parted. He'd changed into jeans and shirt but was still immaculately groomed.

'How did you find out my address?'

'I rang the hospital switchboard while I was waiting for our dinner and they gave it to me. Where would you like to eat? In the kitchen—on the floor—in your bedroom?'

Penny laughed. It was either that or burst into tears.

'How about on the floor in the lounge room?' She pointed him in the right direction while she collected two glasses as he'd also brought a bottle of wine. They ate on either side of the coffee-table, their discussion ranging from international and national politics to movies. Penny was delighted to discover that Sam loved seeing movies on the big screen.

'What about the new Arnold Schwarzenegger film?' Penny asked as she sipped her wine. 'Have you seen it?'

'Not yet. I was planning on seeing it this weekend. If you're free would you like to come with me?'

'I'm on take on Saturday and mop-up on Sunday. On Monday I'm on holidays for the week,' Penny said regretfully.

'I'll let you have a rain-check.' Sam smiled and this time Penny was relaxed enough to respond with her own smile. He started to pack the empty containers away and then pulled Penny to her feet. 'It's almost ten o'clock. Go to bed and I'll see you in the morning.'

Penny walked him to the door. Their eyes held and before she knew what was happening Sam was reaching for her and his lips were pressing hungrily over hers.

Penny felt her heart beat faster as his tongue delved deeply into her mouth. She wound her arms around his neck and pulled his head down to keep it firmly in place. Sam gathered her closer and she felt herself capitulate as he softly groaned her name.

Slowly, ever so slowly, he released her. They stood there for a moment, staring at the desire mirrored in each other's eyes.

'Sleep well. Sweet dreams,' he said before turning and striding away into the darkness of the night.

'Is the professor in?' Penny queried casually of Sam's secretary.

'He's expecting you, Dr Hatfield. Please go straight in.'

Penny put out a hand to open the door to Sam's office, noticing that she was shaking. He had paged her just before eight o'clock and she had been briskly informed that he wanted to see her in his office in five minutes.

I wonder which twin I'll get. The nice one or the horrible one? Penny thought before pushing open the door.

He was working at his desk when she entered. The door closed soundlessly behind her as she walked over to his desk waiting for him to look up but he didn't.

'Remain standing, Dr Hatfield. I won't be a moment.' He continued to scribble more notes down, leaving Penny to wonder what was going on.

Uh-oh. It was the horrible one.

She looked down at him still scribbling on a piece of paper. A lock of black hair had fallen over his forehead and her fingers itched to brush it back into place. She grasped one hand in the other to stop herself from fulfilling the impulse as he finally put his pen down and glanced up at her.

He looked her up and down before pushing his chair back and rising to his feet. Their eyes never breaking contact, Sam extended a hand and reached for one of hers. She let him take it and draw her slightly closer to his white-coated body.

He bent his head to nibble at her earlobe.

'Did you sleep well?'

Struck dumb, Penny could only nod.

'Good,' he said simply and lowered his head to claim her lips in another heart-stopping kiss. The heat in the room seemed to rise to boiling temperature as the kiss intensified.

It seemed to last for ages but in reality it was only a few seconds. This time it was Penny who pulled away, a look of bewilderment mixed with desire on her face.

'Good morning, Dr Hatfield.'

'Sam. What if someone was to walk in?'

He chuckled. 'Well, good morning to you too.'

'Sam. I'm serious.' Penny disengaged herself from his arms and made herself take a few paces backwards.

'Relax. I told my secretary that you and I were not to be disturbed. She wouldn't dare send anyone in.'

'Great. Then she'll really be suspicious.'

'Nonsense.' He dismissed the notion with a wave of his hand then picked up a packet of X-rays. 'There was one other reason that I wanted to see you. First of all, how did you go in Theatre this morning with Mark Shields?'

'Fine. I fixed the kneecap with routine technique. There was only minor damage to the joint surface and it didn't need further attention.'

'Did you use precautions? A man that heavily tattooed has a higher risk of HIV infection.'

'Yes. Naturally he was tested and the test showed negative. I still double-gloved, wore a waterproof

gown, a facial shield. . .you know, the usual precautions.'

'Good. Come and take a look at these.'

She watched as he took the X-rays out of the packet
and switched on his viewing machine.

'Mr Barry Wilson. He's a sixty-four-year-old
married farmer. Fell from a horse then the horse fell
on him.' Sam pulled the X-rays off and hooked the CT
scan with 3D reconstruction views onto the viewer.

Penny moved in closer. 'He has a very comminuted
fracture to the left hemi-pelvis.'

'Which has involved a fracture to the sacro-iliac
joint, acetabulum and pubic rami bilaterally,' Sam
finished off. 'I've booked him for Theatre this afternoon and I would like you to assist me. I know you're
due to be teaching the students but you've had a lot of
exposure to this kind of injury. I need you in that
operating theatre.'

'How do you know about my exposure to pelvic
fractures?'

Sam grinned. 'Can't pull the wool over your eyes,
can I, sweetheart? I was in San Francisco last year at
the academy meeting. I heard your paper on pelvic
fractures and was suitably impressed.'

Penny was stunned. At being called 'sweetheart' and
that Sam had been 'suitably impressed' with her almost
twelve months ago.

'I didn't realise you were at that meeting. In fact, I
checked whether you would be attending and your last
secretary told me you weren't.' Penny blushed at his
interested smile. 'I wanted a chance to meet you and
introduce myself,' she confessed and received an even
greater smile from Sam.

Feeling the blush rise, Penny turned her attention

back to the viewer. 'What technique do you want to use?'

'You're the one who studied with the great French professor. Why don't you tell me, Dr Hatfield?' Sam smiled at her then returned to his chair.

'Open reduction and internal fixation of the left innominate and acetabular fracture. Probably best to use both an ilio-inguinal approach as well as Kocher-Langenbeck approach.' Penny turned from the viewer and seated herself on the other side of Sam's desk. 'Do you have any Plasticine?'

'Why?' he asked, his brow creasing into a frown.

'Pierre always simulated the fracture onto a plastic pelvic model with Plasticine. It's the closest way for the doctor to be able to pick up the patient's pelvis and take a good look at what needs doing.'

'Pierre? Were you always on a first-name basis with the great pelvic fracture specialist?' Sam growled, his frown deepening to a scowl.

Penny smiled sweetly. 'Jealous, Professor Chadwick? Considering he's actually seen me naked, it seems ridiculous to be so formal.'

'What?' Sam exploded, slamming his hands down on his desk. Penny couldn't resist throwing back her head and laughing at him. He definitely made a sight when he was jealous.

'Of course,' she managed to choke out between laughs, 'I was only about nine or ten months old at the time.'

Sam sat back in his chair and crossed his arms defensively. 'I suppose you think you're funny?' he growled.

'I'm sorry.' Penny stopped laughing and wiped the tears from her eyes. 'I couldn't resist that. He's an old friend of my father.'

Sam leaned forward and looked intently into her eyes. 'So, does this mean that because you and I are on a first-name basis with each other that I should see you naked?'

Penny's eyes widened at his suggestion and he chuckled to himself.

Fortunately they were interrupted by a buzzing sound coming from the intercom on Sam's desk. His secretary just wanted to let him know that the weekly X-ray meeting was about to begin.

'Can you get someone to swap your teaching round with you?' Sam stood and gathered up the X-rays.

'Yes. I'll go to Theatre after the meeting and check the equipment. Anything else that you'd like organised?' Penny asked and looked into eyes that never failed to elicit a response from her heart.

'Could you explain the procedure to Mr and Mrs Wilson and put their minds at rest?' He turned to walk out the door but stopped next to Penny. 'There was one other thing I wanted from you.' He quickly bent his head for another electrifying kiss, turned on his heel and walked out the door, leaving her standing in the centre of his office trying to control her emotions.

Now she was definitely confused. Which way was up? she wondered as she followed Sam's footsteps into the meeting.

CHAPTER THREE

'MR AND MRS WILSON, I'm Dr Hatfield and I will be assisting Professor Chadwick with your surgery this afternoon,' Penny began cheerfully after seeing the anxious look on both their faces. 'I've come to explain the injury and surgery to you and to answer any questions you might have.'

Mrs Wilson reached out a hand and her husband held it firmly in his.

'Will Barry make it out alive, Doctor?' Mrs Wilson asked, her eyes watery with unshed tears.

'Of course. There's no reason why he shouldn't. It all sounds so scary being told you've fractured your pelvis, especially when you consider that it's a bone we certainly can't do without. The procedure is complicated but very achievable. There are certain factors that can cause problems in any surgery such as smoking and drinking and being overweight.

'Fortunately for you and us, Mr Wilson, you're very healthy, not carrying any excess weight, and you neither drink nor smoke. Your heart is as healthy as they come and you should have no problems in making a complete recovery. The only problem is that recovery takes time and patience so if you're prepared to help yourself recover you'll be fine.'

Mrs Wilson had dried her tears through Penny's speech and was listening intently.

Penny hooked the CT scan with 3D reconstruction views on the viewer, enabling Mr and Mrs Wilson to see clearly exactly where the fractures were.

'When that horse fell on you, Mr Wilson, it did some considerable damage. The left half of your pelvis has a comminuted fracture, which means that it's broken in several places.' Penny pointed to the different parts as she named them. 'The sacro-iliac joint, the acetabulum and the pubic rami. What we'll be doing is plating and screwing these sections back together so that they're firmly held and the bone can knit and join in the correct places.'

Both Mr and Mrs Wilson were silent for a few moments.

'Well, I feel much better now.' Mrs Wilson squeezed her husband's hand tighter. 'Don't you worry about the recovery part, Doctor. Barry and I will make sure that we follow your orders to the letter.'

'Were there any questions either of you wanted to ask?'

'No. You've put my mind at rest,' said Mr Wilson. 'That Professor Chadwick is a fine fellow as well. I'm sure that between the two of you I'm in good hands.'

'Thank you,' Penny acknowledged. There was a knock at the door—as Mr Wilson had been put into a private room—and the ward sister poked her head around.

'Are you almost finished, Dr Hatfield?'

'Yes.' Penny gathered up the X-rays and scans.

'Good, because Mr Wilson's children and grand-children are waiting to see how he is.'

'Wonderful.' Penny looked at her patient before departing. 'I'll be seeing you later, Mr Wilson.'

'OK. Give me a check X-ray,' Sam ordered. The surgery had gone very well with no complications. Penny and Sam had worked as though they were one person, each assisting the other with barely a word exchanged.

The theatre phone rang and the scout nurse answered it.

'It's your secretary, Professor. She wanted to remind you of the Heads of Department meeting with the State Minister for Health. You've got less than twenty minutes. Do you want her to pass on your apologies?'

Penny, who was standing next to Sam, was the only one to hear him swear. 'No. I'll be there. Tell her to have my files ready. I'll be racing through there in ten minutes. Ask her to call to let them know I'll be five minutes late.' He turned his attention to the operating staff.

'Dr Hatfield, close in layers with number one Vicryl, double zero Vicryl and then staple. I want him in skin traction with three pound weights.' His eyes met Penny's over their masks. Sam cleared his throat and spoke briskly. 'I'll be round to see him this evening. You can give me the update then, Dr Hatfield.'

'Yes, Professor,' Penny acknowledged his request as he turned and left the theatre.

After finishing in Theatre Penny showered and changed before meeting Derek on the ward for a round. Mark Shields was recovering well and would be ready for discharge in another day or so.

'Could you have a word with Mrs Smithers? Her husband's in room two and she has a few questions about the operation you performed the other day.' Derek had grinned devilishly at her as he delivered this information.

Mr Reginald Smithers had undergone a right total hip replacement with no complications but as he suffered from Munchausen's syndrome he worried his wife sick. No wonder Mrs Smithers had some questions.

Penny knew that she'd have to talk to her tonight. Her conscience wouldn't let her get away with it. 'This day will never end.'

'Aww. Poor little Penny's had a bad day. I heard you were summoned to see the professor early this morning before the meeting.'

Penny turned her back on Derek at his mention of 'the professor'. Just the thought of Sam made her tremble. 'Yeah. Then he whisked me off to Theatre for the afternoon.' She tried to keep her tone light as she concentrated on gathering Mr Smithers's file and X-rays.

'You better watch it, Penny. The other guys might get jealous if the professor keeps dragging you away all the time,' Derek laughed and Penny spun round to look at him, her face flushed.

'Was there anyone else I needed to see or is it just Mr and Mrs Smithers?' Her tone was brisk and efficient, causing the smile to slide off Derek's face.

'Hey. Come on, Penny. I was just kidding.' He studied her for a moment longer. 'You really don't like the new professor, do you?'

'Wh-what gave you that idea?' Penny stammered, not quite believing that Derek might be giving her a way out.

'Well, you always seem so nervous at the mere mention of his name. Besides, the way he drilled you out the other day I wouldn't blame you.' Derek draped an arm casually over Penny's shoulders. 'Don't let the guy get to you. Just switch off all personal emotions when working with him and you'll be fine. After all, he's impersonal with all his staff so we may as well be impersonal with him.' He gave her shoulder a little squeeze before turning to leave. 'Although he is an excellent surgeon, don't you think?'

Penny didn't know what to say so she simply nodded. She quickly walked over to room two, banishing all thoughts of the conversation she had just had from her head.

'Good evening.' Penny put on a happy smile for her patient. 'How are you feeling, Mr Smithers?'

'Terrible, Doctor. Just terrible. My foot is in so much pain that I think it's gangrenous.'

'Which foot, Mr Smithers?' Penny placed the file and X-rays on the table before washing her hands.

'The left one, Doctor. I'm so pleased you've come. I was just about to buzz for the nurse.'

Penny lifted the blankets and examined his left foot.

'Will he be all right, Dr Hatfield?' Mrs Smithers asked as she sat on a chair by the bed.

'It looks fine,' Penny announced to both of them.

'Are you sure, Doctor?' Mr Smithers queried.

'Yes. I'll just have a quick look at your hip,' Penny said in an effort to distract him. 'It's healing perfectly, although I think your dressing is due to be changed. Now, Mrs Smithers, I understand you have some questions for me?'

'That's right.'

'Why don't we go into the sister's office to discuss things while one of the nurses changes your husband's dressing?'

'That would be nice.'

Penny collected the file and X-rays and seated Mrs Smithers in the sister's office before ordering an immediate change of dressing for Reginald.

'What seems to be the problem?' Penny asked as she sat down, thankful to be off her feet for a while.

'I know Reginald tends to worry too much about his

injuries but is his hip healing correctly?'

'Yes. He's a textbook case.' Penny pulled out an X-ray and held it up to the light. 'This is his fractured hip a few hours after his fall from the ladder. Old age tends to make our bones very brittle and because your husband is in his mid-seventies he's no exception. We've taken out the fractured bone and replaced it with a metal prosthesis.' Penny held up the post-operative X-ray. 'The operation was straightforward with no complications.'

'But what about his foot? Why is he having pain there?'

Penny sat back in her chair and said softly, 'Do you know that your husband suffers from Munchausen's syndrome?'

'Well, our general practitioner did talk to us about something like that but Reginald did all the talking and, to tell you the truth, Dr Hatfield, I didn't understand most of it.'

'Munchausen's syndrome is a mental disorder in which the patient persistently tries to obtain treatment for an illness that is non-existent.

'Usually patients with Munchausen's syndrome need to have more than one area affected at a time. There was no sign of any damage to his foot. The bone, muscles and tendons all proved normal when I examined it. No doubt over the next few weeks your husband will have quite a number of aches and pains but all of them will be related to Munchausen's syndrome.'

Penny watched as Mrs Smithers relaxed in her chair.

'Hospital-wise, it can be very difficult with Munchausen's syndrome patients because they could be in real pain. That's why every complaint your husband will make *must* be checked by the hospital. We can't afford to pacify him or be blasé. It is a very real disease and he'll need a lot of love and support from you to get him through this.

'I want to make it clear that if you have any other questions ask the nursing staff to page me. You may find that you're the one not coping and if that's the case I don't want you to feel alone.'

Mrs Smithers took a deep breath and expelled it shakily. 'I hope I can cope but I'll be sure to ask for help. Thank you, Dr Hatfield.' She rose out of her chair. 'I'd better get back to Reginald.'

Penny packed up the X-rays and returned them and the file to the ward before going upstairs to the intensive care unit to check on Mr Wilson, the pelvic fracture patient. She wasn't sure what time Sam would be coming back but she'd just have to stay until then.

'How's Mr Wilson doing, Sarah?' Penny asked the night sister.

'He's fine. Blood pressure is a bit low but we're monitoring it closely.'

'Good. Keep him on half-hourly obs until the round tomorrow morning. Is Mrs Wilson still here?'

'Yes. She refuses to go home and she's exhausted.'

'I'll have a word with her. Ring the nurses' home and see if you can get her a bed.' Penny went to Mr Wilson's bedside to find him roused, his wife still sitting by the bed clutching his hand.

'How are you feeling, Mr Wilson? Any pain?' Penny picked up his chart to check his drug intake.

He shook his head, his eyes beginning to close again. Within seconds he was asleep. Penny turned to look at his wife.

'Mrs Wilson, can I get you a cup of coffee or tea?'

'Thank you, I'd like a tea, please,' she said with a tired smile.

'Why don't we go into the sister's office where you can relax for a while? That way we won't disturb your husband.'

Penny ushered her into the small room which was enclosed with glass so that the nurses' station could be seen clearly if anything happened. She made the tea and sat down to talk to Mrs Wilson.

'He looks so frail,' Mrs Wilson said with a sob. 'He's constantly drowsy and. . .I'm so worried.' She let the tears flow. Penny offered her tissues and comforted her.

'It's mainly the general anaesthetic and the analgesic drugs that are making him sleep so much. Over the next few days he'll get his colour back and be his usually happy self again.'

'How long will he need to be in hospital?'

'For about six weeks or so. I'm sure the intern discussed this with you and your husband on arrival?' Mrs Wilson nodded and Penny continued, 'Why don't you get some rest, Mrs Wilson? You've had a very emotional day. I always think it's worse for the person who hasn't gone through the operation. You can't understand what your husband is going through, even if he was to tell you in detail how he was feeling right now. You can't feel the pain or the drowsiness so all you can do is worry about him. That can be more exhausting than the actual operation.'

'I don't want to leave here. I was supposed to stay with my daughter and her family because they're only a half-hour drive from the hospital but even that is too far. I want to stay with him, Dr Hatfield. Just in case. . .'

'I know how you feel. Why don't you go over to the nurses' home and lie down there for a few hours? You'll be minutes away from your husband and I promise I will get the sister to call you if anything should happen.'

'Can you do that?' A faint ray of relief crossed her face.

'Sure. Most times we're in need of sleep but can't be too far away from the patients. So we book a room and go and sleep for a few hours. The nurses' home is the building directly behind this one. You'll do more to help your husband if he sees you bright-eyed and bushy-tailed first thing tomorrow morning.'

'Can I call my daughter and let her know?'

'Certainly. Use the phone in here to give you some privacy.' Penny left and went to have a quick word with Sarah.

'Is Mrs Wilson booked in?'

'Yes.'

'Right. I'll take her across in a few minutes.' Penny checked her watch. It was almost seven o'clock. 'I'm not sure what time the professor is due in but I'll be right back when I've finished with Mrs Wilson.'

Penny was back in ICU within ten minutes. She was deep in discussion with Sarah when she heard footsteps behind her. Expecting to see Sam, Penny was pleasantly surprised to see another familiar face.

'Sir Horace,' Sarah said, smiling broadly, 'it's a pleasure to see you after such a long time.'

Sir Horace shook Sarah's hand. 'The feeling is mutual. I've spent the last hour continually bumping into people I haven't seen for years.'

Penny reached over and gave Sir Horace a kiss.

'So, what brings you here, Dad?'

'Can't an old and retired surgeon come and see his daughter once in a while?'

'Hah! You saw me last weekend. Have you come to see Joss Franklin?'

'Yes. He's picking up quite nicely and is looking forward to returning to the retirement village. He's

missing his friends.' He paused and looked around at
the intensive care patients. 'I can remember spending
the odd night or two up here.' His tone was wistful as
he reached up to adjust the spectacles that sat on his
nose. Sir Horace Hatfield had been one of the world's
leading neurosurgeons until deteriorating eyesight
forced him to retire. Now he and Penny's mother lived
on a property an hour's drive from Adelaide.

'So,' he smiled at his daughter. 'How would you
like to have dinner with your dear old dad? I am right
in assuming that you haven't eaten?'

'Yes and yes.' Penny smiled. 'I just have to wait
for the Prof to arrive, check Mr Wilson and then I'm
free to go.'

'Splendid.' Sir Horace turned to Sarah. 'May I use
your office to sit and wait?'

'Go ahead. Penny's already been using it so you may
as well go in and relax. I'll let the Prof know where to
find you.'

Penny made her father tea and they sat and chatted
about the happenings in the hospital. Half an hour later
Penny could see Sarah motioning to her from the
nurses' station. Penny rushed out and looked to where
Sarah gestured. Sam was standing by Mr Wilson's
bedside, reading his chart.

'He's in a terrible mood,' Sarah whispered. 'He
walked in, barked, ''Where's Dr Hatfield?'' and went
to Mr Wilson's bedside.'

'Terrific. This is just what I need.' Penny took a
deep breath and went over to Mr Wilson's bed.

'Good evening, Professor.' Penny spoke quietly and
Sam turned to glare at her.

'Where have you been?' His voice was low and
demanding.

'In the sister's office.' Penny decided to ignore his

temper and launched into a minute-by-minute account of what had happened to Mr Wilson since Sam had left the operating theatre.

Mr Wilson roused from his drug-induced sleep only to question urgently, 'Where's Margaret?'

'She gone over to the nurses' home to get a few hours' sleep, Mr Wilson,' Penny replied softly. 'She'll be back first thing in the morning.' He smiled weakly at this news and shut his eyes again, his breathing becoming more heavy as he slipped back into slumber.

Twenty minutes later they finished their assessment of Mr Wilson and Sam gently pulled Penny aside.

'Would you like to go and have something to eat?'

Penny stared at him in amazement. He really was a Dr Jekyll and Mr Hyde.

'No, thank you,' Penny replied coldly. 'I already have plans for dinner.' She gestured with her hand toward the sister's office where they could see the back of a man's head.

'Been entertaining your . . *friends* during hospital time, Dr Hatfield?' Before Penny could get a word in to explain exactly who her friend was Sam continued, his eyes ablaze with anger. 'You are not paid to socialise in this hospital. You are paid to perform your duties. I've already told you that I do not appreciate my staff flirting with each other. I won't tolerate it.' His tone was deadly.

'But he's not a staff member,' Penny flustered. 'He's. . .'

'That makes it even worse. Bringing your romantic acquaintances to work is indecent. I will not stand for it, Dr Hatfield. Do I make myself clear?' His blue eyes were venomous.

'Perfectly.' Penny spat the word before he turned and stalked off the ward. She stood, unable to move for a few moments. Sarah came over to her with a box of tissues.

'He really can be a beast at times.' She offered the tissues but Penny was too numb to cry. 'What on earth did he say to you? You're as white as a ghost.'

'You don't want to know.' Penny took a deep breath. 'Right. I think I'll go and have dinner with my father. Thanks for your support, Sarah. I'll see you tomorrow.'

Penny didn't enjoy the meal with her father nearly as much as she wanted to. Sam had put a terrible taste in her mouth and it was hard to get rid of it. She tried to put on a happy face for her father's sake and forget about Samuel Chadwick but it was easier said than done. Her father, bless him, didn't try to talk it out of her.

On the drive home Penny knew that she didn't want to face Sam the next morning. She wanted a chance to explain exactly what had happened. To tell him that it had been her father who had been sitting in the sister's office. That it wasn't a romantic acquaintance, as he had thought.

Who was she kidding? Sam would no more listen to her tomorrow than he would tonight. She'd just have to deal with this in the best possible way. Derek had advised her to be impersonal with him. Well, impersonal and professional she would be. She had already admitted to herself that there was a certain chemistry brewing between herself and Professor Chadwick, although where it might lead she had no idea.

What she found hardest to believe was that she had only known him for three days. Three very *full* days. During those three days she had experienced a multitude of emotions. His kisses were so sweet. His seductive voice, enchanting. His caresses, unforgettable.

She decided, as she pulled into the driveway and made her way inside her townhouse, that she would have to fight fire with fire. Samuel Chadwick deserved to be taught a lesson. She had never flirted with any of her colleagues before but now she decided that it was time to change that. The lucky colleague would be none other than the professor himself.

She'd do it in the most subtle way, of course. Drive him to absolute distraction that he could do nothing about. She grinned as she climbed into bed. Roll on morning.

Penny was up bright and early and dressed for battle. She knew that Sam found her attractive and that he wanted her. Well, she would teach Professor Samuel Chadwick a lesson about wanting.

She wore a lightweight, charcoal linen skirt that was cut just above her knee. Being five feet four meant that she didn't have all that much leg to show but what she did have she was going to drive Sam agonisingly crazy with.

She donned a white embroidered cotton blouse and dug out the plain-lensed glasses she had worn through medical school and her internship.

She pushed gold studs through her ears, then added lip gloss to her full lips and mascara to emphasise her deep, brown eyes. Slipping the glasses onto her nose, she realised that they actually enhanced her facial features and for this she was grateful.

She slipped her feet into low-heeled black court shoes. There was no point in punishing her feet because she was mad at Sam.

She resolved to stay calm and cool toward him but still maintain her professionalism. Penny knew that she looked businesslike but also very, very sexy. Samuel

Chadwick wasn't going to be able to resist her today. But resist he would have to.

She arrived at the hospital and was pulling on her white coat when Derek walked into the registrar's office and let out a whistle.

'Excuse me, but who are you?'

Penny raised her eyebrows, a smirk on her lips.

'You look mysteriously like a colleague of mine,' Derek continued as he walked slowly around her, covering her body with very appraising looks. 'Penny Hatfield is her name, but I haven't seen Penny in a skirt since. . .' he tapped a finger to his chin and rolled his eyes heavenward '. . .since graduation, and even then her mother made her wear it.'

'Very funny, Chalmers. So I felt like dressing up a little. What's the big deal?'

'The big deal is that you look like a woman instead of a doctor. A very seductive woman at that. Why didn't I realise years ago that you might look this good if you took a bath once in a while?' He laughed at his own joke and Penny punched him playfully in the arm.

'If I didn't know you better, Derek Chalmers, I'd say you were making a pass at me.'

'Lucky you know me better, then. But seriously. . .' all traces of laughter died from his face '. . .why the outfit? Trying to impress someone?'

'Wrong. I just felt like a change. As you said, I look like a woman instead of a doctor. So what's wrong with that once in a while? Leave it alone, Derek.' She picked up her stethoscope and gave him a shove toward the door. 'Come on or we'll be late for ward round. We don't want to keep the Prof waiting.'

They walked onto the ward to meet with the other

doctors. Sam was talking to the sister but broke off when they arrived.

'Glad you two could join us,' he said in clipped tones but his gaze lingered on Penny and she watched his eyes travel the entire length of her body in a visual caress before returning to her face. She ignored the reaction it elicited, not letting herself be swayed by it.

She met his eyes defiantly as the rest of the group began to move off toward the first patient. His eyes held a look of desire—of wanting—of needing.

He took a step closer to her and she hardened her heart against his charm.

'I didn't know you wore glasses, Pen?' He smiled briefly, his voice now soft. The look he was giving her was enough to make her melt into his arms on the spot but she took a step back and said calmly,

'There's a lot about me that you don't know, Professor Chadwick. Now, shall we get on with the round?' She held out a hand for him to precede her toward the rest of the staff.

She caught a glimpse of the shutter coming down across his features before he turned sharply on his heel and walked over to the first patient's bed. The game had begun.

During the entire ward round his mood remained black and he was determined to punish Penny for it. He directed all questions sharply at her, not to any of the other staff. Derek tried to jump in once or twice but only received a brisk, 'I didn't ask you, Chalmers,' back from the professor.

Penny, however, was in the mood to retaliate and accepted his challenge without batting an eyelid. She answered all his questions quietly and competently, giving informed and accurate descriptions where necessary. Even the other surgeons on the ward gave her admiring glances.

'You'll do fine in your exams, Dr Hatfield,' Mr Windsor, a senior consultant, told her as they walked toward the ward conference room.

'Thank you, sir,' Penny acknowledged the other surgeon's comment with good grace and smiled up at him. She turned her head, her eyes clashing with hard, cold, blue ones. She looked past the professor and entered the conference room.

The rest of the ward round continued but when the entire group ascended the stairs to the intensive care unit to check on Mr Wilson Penny felt her resolve begin to crumble. Two straight hours of attack from Sam was more than she could take. But take it she would.

'Right, Dr Hatfield, as this is your special patient I suggest you explain the procedure performed yesterday.'

She took the chart from the intern and turned to make her way to the head of the bed where she could face the group and point out the different methods that were used.

'Good morning, Mr Wilson,' she beamed happily at her patient. 'I'm just going to give a brief outline of the surgery that Professor Chadwick and I performed yesterday. You just lie back and enjoy the show and I'll be free to have a chat after we've finished.'

Mr Wilson moved his head slightly in a nodding movement. Penny knew from his chart that he had just received a dose of pethidine. Hopefully he would sleep through the inquisition she was about to get.

'As you would have seen from the X-rays and scans that we viewed downstairs, Mr Wilson had a left innominate and acetabular fracture which required open reduction and internal fixation.'

Penny continued her spiel on the surgery performed yesterday and included the post-operative regime of prophylactic drugs to be issued and traction details. Surprisingly she received little questioning from anyone and within a few minutes of her speech the ward round was concluded.

Derek stayed behind as everyone else drifted off and when Penny had finished making a few extra notes on Mr Wilson's chart he placed a hand under her elbow and ushered her off the ward.

'Where are we going, Derek?' she asked wearily, not having the strength to pull herself away.

'You need coffee, and fast. What on earth have you done to Samuel Chadwick that he hates you enough to put you through that three-ringed circus of a ward round?'

They descended the stairs and entered the registrar's office.

'You don't want to know,' Penny replied despondently as she sank into a chair. She buried her face in her hands as she heard Derek going through the motions of coffee-making.

'Come on, Penny. I've known you for ten years. You're one of my best friends—you can tell me.'

Penny shook her head. 'It would be much better for you if you were kept right out of it. I won't drag you into this private war that Sam and I are having.'

'On a first-name basis with him already?' Derek's voice lost its concern and took on a teasing note.

Penny raised her head as he put a cup of coffee down in front of her.

'My interest is definitely piqued. But, for your sake, I'll leave it. For the moment, anyway.'

'You'll make someone a good wife some day,' she

said with feigned humour in an attempt to change the subject. 'This is great coffee, Derek.'

'So, how about dinner tonight? You're not on call and neither am I, thanks to our gullible colleague, Dr Markum, who is rostered on to do the night shift.'

'I don't think I'd be very good company. Besides, what about Cindy-Lou? I thought you two were a hot item,' Penny teased.

'That's why I want to take you to dinner tonight. She's getting too close, Penny. I need more space. If she knows I'm dating someone else then maybe she'll get the picture.'

'Well, thank you very much. And I thought you were being nice.' She laughed for the first time that day and felt decidedly better. 'OK. I guess I can stand a night out with you but I get to pick the restaurant.'

Derek nodded. 'Just as well I have family money to fall back on with the expensive tastes you have.' He drained his coffee-cup and stood up to leave. 'I've got to go. I'll pick you up at eight.'

Penny stood and took her cup and Derek's to the sink. How come she always got stuck with the dishes?

Penny breathed a sigh of relief. The past three days had been a torment. The tension between Sam and herself had grown unbearable but now she was free. Holidays at last!

She had planned her holidays three months ago and was going to Victoria to spend a week being pampered at her best friend's hobby farm. They had the luxury of country living but only an hour's drive from Melbourne. She longed to ride a horse again. To feel the freedom of riding atop the country hills on a sunny day, the wind blowing softly around her.

Inside she made herself a cup of cocoa and listened

to the messages on her answering machine. She flicked through her mail before dumping it all in the bin.

The drive to Little River was a good one. The weather was fine and Penny took her time, staying overnight in a motel. She pulled into Janey's farm around midday on Tuesday.

'Penny. . .' Janey rushed out to greet her '. . .I can't believe you're finally here. It's been far too long since we saw each other last. Come inside. Craig can get your bags later.'

The two women entered the beautiful home Janey and Craig had spent years renovating until it was just the way they wanted it. Craig was a lawyer in one of Melbourne's most prestigious firms but was on holiday this week, so Janey informed her.

They shared lunch around the large mahogany table, with Janey's and Craig's two daughters. Sally and Jessie, the eight-year-old twins, were off school sick with a mild dose of food poisoning.

'We had take-away last night as I was just too tired to cook and later on they were both up vomiting.' Janey shook her head. The girls asked to be excused from the table and ran outside to play in the sunshine.

'They look like they're over the worst,' Penny laughed. She was pleased that the girls remembered her from her previous trips. 'And you—' Penny looked at Janey who was now seven months pregnant '—look positively radiant. Pregnancy suits you.'

'Well, I was determined to hang onto this one, no matter what,' Janey laughed lightly. She'd had several miscarriages in the past six years and Penny was more than pleased that this baby was doing just fine.

'I'd love to just sit and chat with you, Penny, but I can tell by the drawn lines on your face that you need to have a ride as soon as possible. Why don't you go and saddle up Harem? The girls washed him this morning so he'd be all ready for you to ride.'

'No. Please, Janey. I can ride later. It's OK if we just talk for a while.'

'Go ahead and ride. I've got to get this place cleaned up. Craig is expecting an old school friend to drop by tonight. He's apparently in town for a few days attending a conference. They haven't seen each other for at least ten years so while they're catching up tonight you and I can do the same.'

'Are you sure?'

'I know you too well, Penny.' Janey gave her friend a concerned look. 'Go and ride. It'll whisk the cobwebs away and you'll feel much more relaxed.'

It didn't take Penny long to saddle Harem and soon she was galloping over the meadow that led to the end of Janey's and Craig's property.

Oh, to be able to feel this free all the time. Penny reflected that in the last few days she had pushed herself exceptionally hard and she deserved this break. She urged Harem on further, the warm breeze fanning her skin. This week she would forget about the hospital. She'd forget about Samuel Chadwick. She'd have a wonderful time with Janey and Craig and the girls.

One week of heaven and then she'd return to her living nightmare.

It was almost three hours before she returned to the house. She and Harem had spent a most enjoyable time walking and trotting along.

Penny quickly tended to Harem, brushing him down and organising his feed, marvelling at how quickly she slipped back into a routine she hadn't done for a number of years.

She apologised to Janey for being so long but only

got waved away and told to have a shower. She took her time under the hot spray, enjoying the feeling of not having to account for every minute. She dressed leisurely and made her way to the kitchen to offer her services.

'Everything is under control. Craig's friend has just pulled up outside so if we get the children fed and off to bed as soon as possible we can enjoy ourselves.'

'Sounds wonderful. And Janey. . .' Penny hugged her friend as closely as her pregnant state allowed '. . .thank you.'

'The pleasure is all mine. Come on, let's go meet Craig's friend. You never know, you just might like him.' Janey walked ahead of Penny, down the hallway and into the sitting-room. 'Actually, Craig only told me while you were in the shower that his friend is also a doctor so you two should have a lot to talk about.'

'That's just what I need,' Penny grumbled to herself, but nevertheless put on a smile as they entered the sitting-room.

'Ah. Come and meet my lovely wife, Janey, and her friend.' Craig stood to welcome the women into the room. Penny was still slightly behind Janey so she couldn't see the other man's face. But when she heard his voice there was no mistaking just who Craig's old school friend was.

'And this is Penny. She and Janey have known each other since they were but babes in arms,' Craig joked and Penny felt her world begin to spin as Samuel Chadwick smiled down at her.

CHAPTER FOUR

'I'VE never fainted in my life,' Penny mumbled to the darkened room, feeling disorientated.

'You have now,' a deep voice chuckled and it all came flooding back to Penny with a rush.

'Where are Janey and Craig?' She sat up slowly and looked at Sam's silhouette. She was in her bedroom.

'They're checking on the food and dishing it up. I brought you in here so we could talk without an audience.'

'You carried me?' The thought of being held in those strong, reassuring arms sent a pleasant tingle down Penny's spine. She wished she'd been conscious for it.

'Yes.' She could tell, even without the light, that he was smiling. 'We need to get a few things straight before we return to our hosts.'

'What have you told them so far?' Penny wasn't sure she was going to like it.

'The facts. I'm your boss and we work well together. That we haven't known each other long but that we are friends nevertheless.'

'Friends!' Penny gave a derisive snort of laughter. 'Is that what you call it?'

'Look, unless we put our professional differences behind us the next four days are not going to be relaxing for either of us.'

'What do you mean "the next four days"?' Penny asked warily.

'Craig's asked me to stay for the week and I've accepted.'

'You can't do this to me, Sam. You're supposed to be at a conference.'

'The conference finishes tomorrow.'

'I've had this holiday planned for three months. You can't do this.' Penny buried her head in her hands. She had looked forward to this one-week break for so long and now it was all to be taken away from her.

'Stop being so childish. Why should I give up a chance to spend time with an old friend of mine just because he happens to be married to one of your friends? Penny, I need this break as much as you do and there is a way it can be achieved so we both come out relaxed and happy.' He waited in silence for a few moments.

'You're right,' Penny said quietly. 'I was acting childishly and I apologise. I've just been under such a lot of tension the last few days.'

'Tell me about it,' Sam replied rhetorically. He ran a hand through his hair then said, 'I've got an idea. Wait here a moment.'

He opened the door and went out. A few seconds later there was a knock at the door.

'Come in,' Penny said hesitantly. Sam entered the room and held out a hand. He did not switch the light on and for that Penny was grateful. She felt a little silly but nevertheless stood and took his proffered hand.

'I'm Sam Chadwick, an old school friend of Craig's. You must be Penny, Janey's closest friend.' They shook hands then Sam pulled her into his arms and gave her a hug. The embrace was not sensual but rather that of a friend. 'Come on, let's go join our worried hosts and show them that you're in one piece.'

The four of them had a marvellous evening, swapping old stories and laughing at each other's childhood adventures. This was a side to Sam she would never have seen around the hospital. Here he wasn't Professor Chadwick; he was merely Sam. Another facet to his personality, Penny thought, unable to take her eyes off his face as it lit up with laughter, making him look years younger.

Finally she forced herself to look away. She glanced up at Janey, noticing a very interested expression cross her friend's face. Penny knew she'd be getting an inquisition from Janey in the morning but for now she was happy and enjoying it.

'Is he the reason you were looking so exhausted yesterday?' Janey asked as they sat down to a late breakfast. Sam and Craig had gone to take the girls to school and Janey was making the most of her opportunity alone with Penny.

'Who?' Penny tried to get around the question but Janey laughed.

'You know exactly who I'm talking about. Sam told us that he's your boss and that you're friends but I know you better than that, Penelope Hatfield. Now spill the beans.'

'We are friends, in a way. Oh, I don't know, Janey. It's all too complicated. We work well together but he's too moody for me.'

'How so?'

'One minute he's nice and the next he's horrible. Like Dr Jekyll and Mr Hyde.' Penny finished off her toast and sipped her coffee.

'Maybe there's a reason for his moods,' Janey said softly and Penny had the distinct feeling that she knew more than she was letting on. 'Anyway, I was watching you two last night and there is some serious chemistry going on.' Janey stopped eating her fruit and looked intently at Penny. 'Has he kissed you yet?'

'Oh, for heaven's sake, Janey.' Penny stood up and began clearing the table. Janey laughed as though they were back in primary school. 'You know,' Penny chuckled, unable to resist Janey's infectious laughter, 'if I had a dollar for every time you've asked me that question I'd be rich.'

'Remember old Simon Prose from primary school?' Janey giggled again.

'You mean Slimy Simy? Yes, I remember. You dared me to kiss him and promised me your allowance of one whole dollar if I did.' Penny shook her head as she reminisced. 'The time and place were set—Friday afternoon behind the shelter shed. You were waiting for me by the gate and I will never, ever forget the way you were so excited that you yelled at the top of your lungs as I was running away from him, "So, Penny, did you kiss him?"'

Janey was laughing so hard that her eyes were watering. Sam and Craig chose that moment to enter, both of them smiling at the sound of Janey's laughter.

'What's so funny?' Craig asked, offering his wife a tissue.

'You still owe me that dollar, Janey,' Penny said with a sassy grin and this only made Janey laugh louder. 'Now let me see how much that would be with inflation.'

Penny looked at Sam through smiling eyes to find him assessing her. She sobered immediately and turned to plug the kettle in.

'I didn't pay you the dollar because you never answered my question. Either of them,' Janey said with a twinkle in her eye.

'We'll discuss it later, Janey. Now, who would like a cup of coffee?' Penny busied herself in the kitchen.

'Come on, you two,' Craig teased. 'Why do you owe

Penny money?' He walked to the back of his wife's chair and began massaging her shoulders.

'Mmm. That feels wonderful. Sam, what time do you have to be at your conference?' Janey tactfully changed the subject, for which Penny was grateful.

'I'll be leaving in about twenty minutes. I've organised for a taxi to come and pick me up and I should be back around sixish this evening.' Sam came and sat down at the table opposite Janey. He was dressed in jeans and shirt and looked gorgeous. Penny had to force herself to concentrate on making the coffee.

'Don't be ridiculous, Sam. I'll take you into town,' Craig offered but Sam held up a hand to decline.

'It's much too far. I'm more than happy to go by taxi.'

'That's a great idea, Craig.' Janey ignored Sam's refusal. 'We can all go into town. Penny and I can do some shopping and you, my darling husband, can carry the bags. What do you think, Penny? You said you wanted to go shopping while you were here.'

'Fine.' Penny forced a smile. She had been looking forward to escaping Sam's presence as soon as possible. She was finding it difficult to relax around him. Not because he was her demanding boss but because the feelings of desire that she had been trying to quell were building up to bubbling point.

Seeing him here, totally at ease with their friends and with his true self shining through, evoked the most incredibly strong feelings of. . .of what? Not wanting to discover the answer to that question, Penny excused herself on the pretence of changing her clothes. She stayed in her room, dressed for the hot weather in a cool, cotton shirt and shorts with comfortable shoes, until it was time to leave.

As she had suspected would happen, Penny was left

to sit in the back seat of the Bentley next to Sam who had changed into a charcoal grey suit and looked every inch the professional he was. They chatted about the conference, who the guest speakers were and what new material was being presented.

Penny was finding it difficult to connect this man, who was definitely the professor, and the Sam they'd all had dinner with last evening. Was she like this as well? Did she have two sides to her personality—one professional, one social?

'What are you planning on buying today, Penny? There's no point in me buying anything because nothing fits,' Janey complained.

'Sure there is,' Craig said, reaching over to squeeze his wife's hand. 'If you go to a tent shop you're bound to find something to fit.' They all laughed and Janey playfully punched her husband in the arm. The laughter eased the tension and from then on Janey and Craig kept up a steady banter.

They reached the convention centre and pulled in to drop Sam off. He thanked Craig for the lift and before getting out of the car turned to look at Penny. His appearance may have said that he was all business but the look in his eyes was one of desire. Penny flushed, embarrassed that he could set her body on fire with just one look.

He cleared his throat. 'See you all later this evening.' He shut the door after him and soon Craig was pulling out into the traffic.

Penny had forgotten what it was like to go shopping with Janey. It was a whirlwind experience that one had to see to believe.

'Come on, Penny. It's perfect. Tell her, Craig.' Janey held the simple black evening dress up in front of Penny.

'It will look stunning on you, Penny,' Craig smiled at her.

'Try it on. Please?' Janey begged. 'If not for yourself, try it on for me so I can see what it would look like on a skinny person.'

'I'd forgotten you had your PhD in shopping,' she mumbled as she entered the change cubicle. Minutes later a transformed Penny appeared in front of her friends. The black crêpe sheath skimmed the length of her body with one large split up the front to mid-thigh. Craig let out a wolf whistle as Penny paraded in front of them with a giggle.

'Oh, Penny. That's just beautiful.' Janey ran her hands over the wide straps of material on Penny's shoulders. 'You've got to buy it.'

'Where would I wear it, Janey?' Penny laughed. 'While I'm doing my rounds? Or, better still, why don't I wear it when I sit my Fellowship exams next year? A sexy dress like this is bound to get me through.'

'We'll go out to dinner while you're here. That will surely knock Sam's socks off,' Janey said with a nod of satisfaction.

Penny blushed, before hotly denying, 'I don't want to knock Sam's socks off or anyone else's for that matter. Why do you have to match-make me up every time I come to see you?' An exasperated Penny went back into the changing-rooms and reappeared as her normal self.

'I'm sorry,' Janey said softly.

'No, you're not. I know you very well, Janey, and you just want everyone to be as happy as you and Craig are.' Penny gave her friend's hand a little squeeze to reassure her before handing over her credit card to the sales assistant. Craig had remained quiet through the last few minutes of conversation and for this Penny was grateful. She had no doubt in her mind that Craig knew exactly what Janey was up to with her supposed match-making. They finished their shopping and headed back to Little River in time to pick the girls up from school.

Penny was outside with Sally and Jessie playing tag while Craig and Janey took care of the meal preparations. Penny was 'it' and was chasing the two squealing girls all over the yard. Sally was the slower of the two and had been caught numerous times so Penny was aiming her sights on Jessie.

They both ducked and weaved in and out of the trees and bushes and finally Penny managed to catch her, enveloping her in a hug. Sally, in her enthusiasm, came racing over, throwing her arms around both Penny and her sister. The three of them were laughing too hard to hear a car rolling up the long driveway and coming to a stop at the front door.

They overbalanced and landed heavily on the grass, Penny now tickling both girls at once and watching them squirm with laughter on the ground. Sam came around to the back door, tie loosened, briefcase still in hand.

'Sam!' Sally squealed with delight, alerting Penny and Jessie to his presence. Soon Penny was left lying on the grass by herself as the twins begged for hugs and kisses. He looked so natural surrounded by children, Penny thought as she propped one hand underneath her head to watch them.

She wondered what colour eyes their children would have—blue or brown? Whoa! She shook her head and scrambled up off the grass. She'd better stop these thoughts before they went too far.

'So how did it go?' she asked as she sauntered over to them.

'There was some very interesting material presented.' His eyes gleamed with excitement. 'Let me get changed and I'll tell you all about it.' He turned his attention to the girls. 'I can tell the two of you are feeling better. Is it almost time for dinner? I'm starving.' He rubbed his stomach. The twins raced inside to enquire about dinner.

It wasn't until after dinner and the girls had gone off to watch some television before bed that Sam finally had the opportunity to tell Penny about the conference.

'They always save the best presentations until the last day so I was pleased that I went today,' Sam announced to the table and then turned to look at Penny. 'A paper was presented on external fixators that will change orthopaedic surgery for ever.' Sam's eyes twinkled with enthusiasm and Janey let out a groan.

'If you two are going to talk shop Craig and I will get the dishes out of the way.' Janey dragged her husband out of the room, leaving Sam and Penny alone. Immediately Sam began telling Penny of the interesting techniques and instruments he had heard about and seen that day at the conference.

Twenty minutes later Janey stuck her head around the corner to inform them that coffee was served. Penny was now as excited as Sam, although part of her happiness was that Sam had shared the information with her. Whenever she had exciting 'medical' news she'd discuss it with her father. Even though he was a neurosurgeon it was good to discuss it with someone who really understood.

She wondered if Sam had anyone he usually talked to? Were his parents doctors? Did he have any brothers or sisters? Did he have a girlfriend? Penny realised that she knew nothing about him but that he already knew quite a lot about her.

Both Sam and Penny were called upon to read bed-time stories to the girls and to tuck them in. Switching off the television, the four of them spent the evening talking about various topics. They made plans to go for a picnic the following day and began discussing what food they would take, what time they would leave and where exactly they'd go.

Janey was tired after their shopping expedition and decided to go to bed early. Craig went too, leaving Penny and Sam alone. They talked softly for a while, mainly about the conference, and when Penny was having difficulty hiding a yawn she decided it was time to turn in.

Sam walked with her down the passageway to her bedroom door, opposite his own. 'Thanks for telling me about the conference, Sam. It was exciting to hear about the new information.' Penny's voice was a whisper, although she bravely kept her eyes focussed on Sam's while she spoke. There was something between them tonight. Something that had never been present before. Was it trust? Penny wasn't sure.

'Thank you for listening. It was good to be able to come home and discuss my excitement with someone who actually understood what I was saying.' He smiled down at her, making her knees go weak. So he didn't have anyone to discuss things with, she thought briefly before leaning against the door for support. She knew that he was going to bestow another heart-stopping kiss on her eager lips.

At first his lips were soft and gentle, teasing her with little butterfly kisses. His hands came up to cup her face as he looked down into the brown depths of her eyes.

'Oh, Pen,' he whispered, 'you are one dangerous

lady.' He lowered his head before she could utter a word and took her lips in an abandoned frenzy. His lips coaxed hers to part as he slipped his tongue into her mouth. Penny opened her lips, groaning softly as she surrendered her inhibitions.

His hands slid down her body to draw her closer at the waist. She raised her arms and locked them around his neck. Slowly she began to rake her fingers through his hair, bringing all her senses to life.

Sam gathered her closer to his muscular frame, pressing her breasts hard against the wall of his chest. Penny could feel his erratic breathing matching her own as her tongue meshed with his, tasting the sweetness of him.

A sudden coughing coming from the girls' room stopped them in their embrace. Neither of them moved for at least a minute. Penny rested her head on his shoulder, trying to control her emotional turmoil.

Slowly Sam raised her chin so that he could look at her, his other arm still clamped firmly around her waist.

'We'd best get some sleep.' His voice was soft but still husky with desire. His eyes belied his words, saying that he would rather whisk her off to either bedroom and finish what they had started.

Penny wanted him to follow through on his impulses but knew the time wasn't right. She smiled at him. 'I doubt if either of us will sleep but I guess we'd better try.'

He reached behind her to open the door, bending his head to brush his lips across hers one more time. Then he gently pushed her inside the room before quietly shutting the door.

*　　*　　*

'Oh, boy! I'm full.' Janey laid back against her husband and rubbed her swollen stomach, a satisfied grin on her face.

'I'm not surprised,' Craig laughed. 'You've eaten most of the sandwiches, not to mention the fruit salad.'

'Stop exaggerating.' Janey joined in his laughter.

'Can you fit a cup of tea in, Janey?' Penny asked as she reached for the Thermos of hot water.

'You'd better believe it.' Craig followed suit and patted his wife's stomach. 'The little fella in here loves his cup of tea. I've had to make her cups of tea at two o'clock in the morning.'

'How can you be sure it's a boy?' Sam asked his friend as he helped Penny unpack the tea, coffee, milk and sugar from the picnic basket. 'Maybe you'll get your wish after all and be surrounded by four beautiful females.'

Janey closed her eyes briefly and clenched her jaw, then took a breath and relaxed.

'You all right, Janey?' Penny asked, watching her friend closely.

'Just a bit of indigestion. I ate gherkin last night when I shouldn't have. Yes, it's definitely a boy,' Janey murmured. 'I can just feel it.'

'Could you ''feel it'' with the girls?' Sam asked casually. 'Or was it too crowded to feel anything but discomfort?'

Janey chuckled. 'We knew in advance that it was two girls—the doctors told us. We decided that with twins it was better to know beforehand so we could be better prepared. The nursery was complete and we had plenty of lovely dresses all ready and waiting for them when we arrived home from the hospital.'

Penny handed around the teas and coffees then began packing the food away.

'It's such a glorious day,' she sighed as she stretched out on the blanket. They had left the house just before eleven o'clock and walked for about half an hour until they had reached Janey's favourite picnic spot.

An enormous gum tree provided them with shade from the hot February sun and although the grass was dry it added rather than detracted from the scenery. Spreading out a huge red and black picnic blanket, Janey had proceeded to unload the food that she and Penny had spent the morning preparing. Craig leant back against the tree trunk so that Janey could be more comfortable leaning on him.

'Sam, could you pass me my cross-stitch? It's in the basket,' Janey asked. 'Once I'm finally comfortable I don't like to move because I can never get comfortable again.'

Sam obliged and then lay down on his side, one hand propped under his elbow as he and Craig talked in hushed tones. Penny gave a small yawn before closing her eyes and dozing.

She awoke to a gentle pressure on her lips and, without opening her eyes, she smiled and stretched languorously, her body coming into contact with one of pure, lean male.

'Mmm. What a nice way to wake up.' Her voice was husky and for a moment she wasn't sure whether she was dreaming or whether the man beside her was real.

'I'll try to remember that.' Sam's drawl had her eyes snapping open as she remembered where she was. She sat up quickly, too quickly, making her head spin.

'Where are Janey and Craig?' She glanced at her watch. She'd dozed for almost an hour.

'Relax. They've gone for a stroll. Janey needed to stretch her legs.'

'Oh,' was all she could say. They were alone and

she had just wantonly pressed her body against his. Embarrassed, Penny began to stand up but two hands firmly clamped themselves around her waist and pulled her back down onto the blanket. He settled her on her side, facing him.

'We've got some unfinished business to discuss.' His voice was husky and Penny could tell from his eyes that he didn't mean anything medical. His eyes burned with the intensity of a furnace as they leisurely travelled the length of her body. Her T-shirt was taut across her heaving breasts and had come untucked from her shorts when she had stretched.

'Pen—' his eyes finally came to rest on hers '—I want you. I can't deny what I feel and I know you feel it too.' His voice was hypnotic. Deep and full of desire. Penny could feel herself beginning to tremble as he ran a hand over her bare arm, the action causing her flesh to goose-bump.

Without breaking eye contact, Sam's hand travelled down to her thigh, up under her T-shirt to the centre of her flat stomach, finally coming to rest on her breast. Slowly his fingers began to work their magic, stirring the blood in Penny's veins.

He shifted downwards so that his mouth could claim the rosy peak, suckling it sweetly. Penny tipped her head back in delight and grasped his head between her hands, making sure he didn't break the contact. . .not just yet.

With one swift movement Sam was above her. His head descended toward her lips for another searing onslaught. By now Penny was lost as wave after wave of desire flooded through her body.

'Pen,' he murmured between kissing her neck and her lips, 'I've dreamt of this ever since I laid eyes on you. I want you.'

'Oh, Sam. I want you too,' she gasped before his tongue delved deeply into her mouth once more, promising to take them to the heights of fulfilment.

'Sam! Penny!' Craig's distressed voice penetrated their passionate haze and they both sat up to see him running toward them. Penny would have been totally embarrassed if she hadn't stopped to take in Craig's pale face.

'Where's Janey?' Penny said calmly although she felt like screaming. She could feel something was wrong.

'Down near the creek. She's been sick and is in an awful lot of pain. She thinks she's in labour.'

CHAPTER FIVE

'WELL, there's no time to lose. Penny, you get things ready here while Craig and I collect Janey and bring her back.' Sam was quick to take charge, all signs of their earlier passion totally erased. Penny nodded and delved into the picnic basket.

She checked the Thermos of hot water, discovering that there would be just enough for sterilising procedures. She tossed the remaining fruit salad from the bowl and wiped it out with a paper serviette. It would be easier for them to wash their hands with the water in a bowl.

Next she emptied the container that held the left-over sandwiches and rinsed and wiped it out. This container had a lid and would be the right size to hold the afterbirth so that they could get it to the hospital for a thorough examination. All the while she worked Penny prayed that it would be a false alarm and that Janey would carry until full term. She should have known that something was wrong when Janey had complained of indigestion. Nevertheless, it was too late to admonish herself now.

She looked at her surroundings. They would need something to tie the umbilical cord with. She checked in Janey's cross-stich box and found plenty of cottons and a fine pair of sharp embroidery scissors.

Clearing everything except what she needed off the blanket, Penny could now only wait for their return. It wasn't long before she saw the two men carrying Janey quickly toward her. They deposited her gently onto the blanket, where Penny quickly reached for her friend's wrist.

'Waters have broken,' Sam informed her.

'Pulse is steady,' she said aloud to reassure herself if no one else. 'Janey, couldn't you feel the contractions getting closer?' She spoke softly to her friend.

'I thought it was just bad indigestion,' Janey panted. 'I had a Caesarean with the girls, remember. I've never had a labour before.' Tears sprang into her eyes and Penny quickly reassured her friend that everything was going to be all right.

'Not to worry. You've got two fine orthopaedic doctors here so if the baby has a broken leg we'll be able to fix it straight away.' Penny brushed the hair back from Janey's forehead before standing to look at Sam. Craig was still kneeling beside his wife, holding her hand tightly.

'Craig, you'll need to go back to the house and get a few things for us.' Sam crouched down beside the frantic man.

'I won't leave Janey,' he vowed, shaking his head.

'Craig.' Penny's voice was soft and reassuring. 'We need you to go back to the house and bring some new newspaper—today's if you can find it—and that big basket of fresh ironing I saw in the laundry. You've got a phone in the car so we can call the hospital once you get back here.' She paused and took Janey's pulse again.

'She's not going to have this baby for at least another hour and by then you'll be back. Craig, it's important that you go. Sam and I can't leave her.' She placed a hand under Craig's elbow and gently urged him to his feet.

'It's OK, Craig. This baby wouldn't dare come into this world without his father there to see it.' Janey smiled weakly at her husband before he bent to kiss her.

He took a deep breath. 'Freshly ironed laundry, new newspaper—anything else?'

'A few blankets, a cake of soap and a hot-water bottle. Everything will be fine.'

Craig nodded before turning and running toward the house. It would take him at least twenty minutes to get there if he ran the entire way.

'What next?' Janey asked, her breathing easing between contractions.

'We wait,' Penny said, sitting down next to her friend and holding the hand that Craig had reluctantly released.

Forty-five minutes later Janey was fully dilated and there was still no sign of Craig. The contractions were only minutes apart and Janey's forehead was bathed in a heavy sheen of sweat.

'Let's scrub, Dr Hatfield,' Sam said quietly. Penny poured the hot water into the bowl and as Sam began to scrub she heard the sound of the Land Cruiser coming closer.

She rushed over to unload after Craig had stopped the car and scrambled over to his wife's side. Quickly passing the soap to Sam, she sorted out the items she needed. The ironing was mainly pillowcases and tea towels, for which Penny was grateful. She quickly placed one underneath Janey, forming a sterile area.

Sam finished scrubbing and bent down next to Janey, telling her what was going to happen. He also told Craig what he must do to help Janey through. Penny felt a momentary pang of jealousy. Janey and Craig were so much in love and about to bring another child into the world. She only hoped that one day it would happen to her.

She quickly placed the scissors into the hot water before thrusting her own hands in to scrub. Setting out her 'instruments' on another ironed pillowcase, Penny was ready. She and Sam exchanged a look that needed no words to accompany it. Regardless of what their differences were, or what had happened just prior to Janey's premature labour, she and Sam were doctors and they had a job to do.

Moments later the baby's head was visible and with a few pushes a slippery little boy made his way into the world.

'You were right, Janey. It's a boy.' His tone was matter-of-fact and Penny could tell that he was concentrating on the task at hand.

With no modern technology around, Sam quickly cleaned out the baby's nostrils and throat the best he could then swung him upside down by his feet and smacked his bottom.

Nothing!

Penny went to work on the umbilical cord as Sam quickly began giving the baby artificial respiration. Everyone present was holding their breath. She stripped back the cord as hard as she could with her fingers and was reaching for the scissors when a spluttering cry came from the small life held firmly in Sam's hands.

For a moment time seemed to stand still before Craig gave a whoop of joy and Janey burst into tears. Penny quickly absorbed herself in what she was doing as she worked the small but sharp scissors through the tough umbilical cord.

'What are you going to call him?'

'David,' Janey said weakly through her tears.

The cord cut, Penny reached for the cotton and, passing one piece to Sam, they each tied off an end. Sam motioned for her to take the baby from him as he got ready to deliver the afterbirth. She wrapped little David in the newspaper before wrapping him in a blanket. She handed him to Janey before placing the hot-water bottle between Janey's arm and the baby, then wrapped a blanket around both of them.

'I know you're going to swelter, Janey, but he's got to be kept as warm as possible. I'll quickly put everything in the car and we'll be on our way.'

She cleared up while Sam delivered the afterbirth, giving it a brief examination before placing it in the container Penny had prepared.

Soon they were all bundled into the Land Cruiser. Sam made Craig drive as he knew the fastest route to Geelong Hospital while Penny and Sam sat in the lowered back seat with Janey and David.

Sam reached for the phone as Craig broke every speed limit and ran every red light. It would take them at least twenty minutes to get there, even at this speed, but the hospital would be waiting for them. He also contacted Janey's specialist and arranged for him to meet them at the hospital.

'The baby and the afterbirth look fine but I'd say he's only about four pounds, if that.' Sam spoke into the receiver with authority.

Penny was constantly checking and rechecking David's breathing, his pulse and his temperature. Janey was sweating as she cradled her son protectively, her eyes closed in exhaustion. Penny kept a close eye on her, murmuring every so often that things were normal.

The hospital staff were fast and efficient as the Land Cruiser screeched to a halt in the emergency bay. Janey and David were bundled onto a stretcher while Craig ran alongside. Penny and Sam were met by Janey's specialist, Dr Matthews—a short and tubby man in his late fifties—and, after giving him a brief but accurate description of the past two hours' events, they were shown to a small waiting-room. Penny glanced at her watch, noticing that it was almost time for school to finish.

'I'd better ring Janey's neighbour to see if she can look after the girls until we arrive home. I'll go and find a telephone.'

After organising the girls' care, she purchased two cups of coffee from the vending machine and walked back to the waiting-room. Sam was sitting heavily in a chair, holding his head between his hands.

'Are you OK?' she asked quietly, going over to sit beside him. 'I've brought you a cup of coffee.' She offered the cup but realised that Sam wasn't listening. His breathing was ragged and for a moment she thought he was crying.

Placing the cups on the floor, Penny hesitantly put a hand on his shoulder. 'Do you want to talk about it?' she asked softly, her heart going out to him. Something was terribly wrong for Sam to be reacting like this.

'Is it Janey or David?' A moment of panic swept over her before Sam looked at her and shook his head. His eyes were devoid of tears—instead they reflected great pain and sorrow.

'What's wrong, Sam?' Penny whispered, unsure of whether she really wanted to know.

He stood and stretched his legs. He turned to face her and, after taking a deep breath, he said, 'It's something that happened to me fourteen years ago. Today just brought the memories flooding back. You see, Penny, I was. . .'

'Well, congratulations—to both of you,' Dr Matthews said, entering the little waiting-room. Sam spun around at the sound of his voice.

'If you hadn't been there today,' he continued, 'both Janey and little David would have died. Marvellous piece of work, especially considering your equipment—or lack of it.'

'They're both fine?' Penny had stood when the specialist had entered, part of her pleased that they had been interrupted. She wasn't sure if she was ready for Sam's confidences yet, even though her compassionate side had wanted him to open up to her so that she could comfort him and help him exorcise his ghosts.

'Yes. Come and see them. I think the one we need to worry about is poor old Craig,' he chuckled as he led the way.

Janey was sitting up in bed while Craig was slumped in a chair. David was in the intensive care nursery in an incubator.

'How are you feeling?' Penny asked as she went to hold Janey's hand.

'Thanks to the two of you, we're all going to be fine.'

'Good. Now I want you to get some rest. You, too, Craig. We'll see if we can get another bed brought in for you,' Sam ordered as he came around to kiss Janey lightly on the forehead. 'Penny's contacted your neighbour and she'll be looking after the girls until we get there. We'll feed them and bring them in to see you later this evening. So make sure you're both rested and relaxed.'

Janey smiled. 'We don't know how to thank you enough.'

'Get some rest,' Penny smiled back. 'We'd better be going. Give me a list of the things you'd like brought in.'

Sam got the keys from Craig as Penny wrote a quick list. On their way out of the ward Sam asked the sister for an extra bed to be placed in Janey's room.

Between his natural charm and authority there was no argument.

The next few days passed in a flurry of excitement. Both Sally and Jessie were ecstatic with their new baby brother and by Saturday Craig and Janey were home. David was to stay in hospital for at least another six weeks but just the joy of his presence was enough to make everyone disregard the inconvenience of the daily trips to the hospital.

On Saturday afternoon Penny said her farewells and bundled her car up with her belongings. 'Why do I always seem to take home twice as much as I came with?' she asked Janey laughingly.

'Thanks again.' Janey hugged her close, a tear escaping down her cheek.

'Hey, don't start,' Penny joked, tears already springing to her own eyes. 'This is what friendship is all about. I'll be there for you and you'll be there for me.'

'Not during your childbirth, I hope.' Janey laughed before waving her friend off.

Penny had a lot to reflect on while driving back to Adelaide. Sam was booked on Sunday morning's flight and had even offered to cancel his flight to drive back with Penny. Somehow she had convinced him that she would be fine and promised to stay overnight in a motel. She was relieved that Sam had accepted this as the close proximity of him in her car for the entire seven-hour drive would have sent her spine-tingling emotions into overdrive.

She was having a difficult time coping with the past forty-eight hours. She and Sam had picked the girls up from the neighbours and had fed and bathed them before taking them to the hospital.

The next morning Penny had fed them breakfast and

done their hair and Sam had taken them to school. It was as though they'd been a real family. Sharing domestic bliss with Samuel Chadwick was something Penny was certain she could get used to, given the chance.

Her mind had wondered again and again about what he had almost told her in that small waiting-room. She kept telling herself that it had nothing to do with her. Sam was a work colleague and. . .a friend? Was he a friend? They had certainly been friends while they were in Little River.

Derek was a work colleague and a friend but Derek didn't make her feel like she was coming apart at the seams when he looked at her. Derek didn't make her want to throw all reason to the wind and go with her instincts. Derek didn't make her heart race, her knees knock, nor did he elicit such a fiery and passionate response as Sam had when he had held her in his arms and kissed her senseless.

She switched on some music to stop that train of thought.

Hearing someone crooning something about love being in the air, Penny immediately tried to switch stations. Unfortunately that was the only station she could pick up.

Penny was back on the ward first thing Monday morning, feeling relaxed and refreshed. She had stopped agonising over her feelings for Sam or how he would react when he saw her next. He was as unpredictable as the weather.

She was sitting in the nurses' station filling out case notes when she heard angry footsteps coming down the corridor. She looked up to see a tall, red-haired man, who was built like an ox, striding past with a very determined look on his face.

She watched as he went over to Maureen Brooker's bed, glaring down at the woman who had now shrunk beneath the bed covers, trying to make herself invisible. Having her broken femur in traction as well as her right arm heavily weighted with the plaster, Maureen was defenceless.

Penny sprang to her feet and rushed over. Maureen was in a ward with five other women and Penny wasn't going to let him frighten all of the other patients the way he was frightening Maureen. Using her white coat as a suit of armour, Penny picked up Maureen's chart.

'Good morning, Maureen. How are you feeling this morning?' Penny had already done her round for that morning but this hairy monster didn't know that. She ignored him completely as she gently prised Maureen's white-knuckled hand from the bedclothes to calmly take her pulse. It was sky-rocketing. She had to get this oaf out of here and fast.

'Excuse me, sir, but visiting hours haven't begun. If you would like to make your way to our waiting-room, I'll have the sister call you as soon as I've finished with Mrs Brooker.' Penny kept her voice calm and soothing. She motioned for the sister to come over and began pulling the curtain around Maureen's bed.

'Sister will show you the way to the waiting area, Mr. . .?' Penny waited intently for the oaf to speak.

'Brooker.' He bared his teeth in what Penny could only guess was supposed to be a smile. 'I'm her husband.'

Penny faltered for a moment as Maureen had told them that she had no family or contacts and that her husband had died.

'It makes no difference to me who you are,' Penny

stated stiffly. 'I am about to examine my patient and therefore you must leave, Mr Brooker. Sister will escort you.'

For a moment Penny didn't think her ploy had worked but Mr Brooker grunted once more before turning abruptly, ignoring the relieved sister, and made his way noisily out of the ward.

Maureen was as white as a ghost and was trembling as though she had seen one. Penny knew she had to calm her down before she became hysterical.

'Was that man your husband?' Penny asked firmly. Maureen turned widened eyes her way and nodded hurriedly.

'Why did you tell me he was dead?' Penny scribbled something on a piece of paper and handed it to the sister, who scuttled off, leaving Penny alone with her patient.

'I wish he was dead.' Maureen found her voice at last but even then it was only a scared whisper.

'Do you want to see him?' Penny asked, her tone more gentle.

'No. I don't. I want to stay in here for ever. The hospital can protect me and that way he can't hurt me.' Maureen began to sob and Penny placed a sympathetic hand on her patient's shoulder.

'It's all right. I'll make sure he is restricted from the hospital but you'll have to leave here eventually, Maureen.'

Maureen shook her head miserably. Penny offered her a tissue, watching the frightened woman with concern.

'I'd like you to talk to one of our social workers.'

'No. I don't want to talk to anyone, except. . .maybe you, Dr Hatfield.'

'Maureen. You are making yourself sick with worry

and that means that your fractures are going to take longer to heal than necessary. I know you feel secure in hospital but that isn't going to solve your problems. You'll need a lot of help when you leave here and the social worker can assist in this, whereas I can't.'

Penny looked at her patient again, a feeling of sadness sweeping over her.

'Dr Hatfield,' Maureen sobbed quietly, 'he was the one who pushed me down the stairs.' Penny let her patient cry for a little while, relieved that Maureen was going to open up and let her help.

The sister came in to the enclosed area, bringing with her the medication Penny had requested.

'Sister,' Penny addressed her colleague in a hushed whisper, 'have Carol come around immediately and also arrange for Mrs Brooker to be transferred to a private room.'

'Yes, Dr Hatfield.'

'Could you also contact the professor? I'll need to speak to him as well.' Penny turned her attention back to Maureen.

'How long has he been abusing you, Maureen?' Her tone was gentle but firm.

'For about the past two years. Usually when he's been drinking.' Maureen stopped crying and blew her nose.

'How do you feel now?' Penny once again checked her patient's pulse, which was returning back to normal.

'I can feel a headache building up.'

'I'm not surprised.' Penny smiled softly. 'I've prescribed something for you which will let you sleep a little and will also relieve the headache but I don't want you to have it until after you've spoken with Carol. She's the social worker who's. . .'

'Here.' Carol poked her head through the curtain and smiled at the two women. Penny made the introductions before the sister came to tell her that she was needed on the phone. Penny collected the prescribed drugs off Maureen's table and returned them to the sister with her instructions.

'Dr Hatfield.' She spoke into the receiver, breathing a sigh of relief that Maureen's floodgates had opened and that she would at last let people help her.

'I hear you've been after me?'

There was no mistaking the smooth, masculine voice on the other end of the phone and Penny's knees gave way immediately. Fortunately for her she landed on the stool. The double meaning in his words was enough to make her blush and she turned her head in case someone should notice.

She cleared her blocked throat. 'Yes, Professor. It's Maureen Brooker. She told the intern who took her history that she had no family and that her husband was dead. He's turned up here this morning, alive and well and looking extremely dangerous. I managed to get him to leave the ward and I assume he went to the waiting-room, as per my suggestion.' Penny stopped for breath.

'Mrs Brooker then confessed that her husband was the person who pushed her down the stairs and has been abusing her for the last two years or so. She would like him kept away from the hospital and Carol is with her at the moment.' She paused for a moment before adding more quietly, 'That's why I've been after you.'

She heard Sam take a deep breath then expel it. 'I'm still at home but it won't take me long to come in. Check to see if Mr Brooker is in the waiting-room. If so, contact Security and have him escorted off the hospital grounds. Chances are he's already left and if that's the case I'll contact Security and the police department when I arrive. I should be there in about ten minutes. I'll meet you in the ward.'

Sam was correct. Mr Brooker had left the hospital and for this Penny was relieved. She had only witnessed someone being escorted off hospital grounds once before and she didn't really want to see it again.

She knew that Carol would be working miracles with Maureen Brooker, getting her to open up and to know that she could do something about an abusive husband. Carol was a brilliant social worker and this was yet another time that Penny was thankful to have her on the orthopaedic wards.

While she waited for Sam, Penny made herself a cup of coffee and went back to writing her reports in the case notes. She was trying extremely hard not to dwell on the fact that she would be seeing Sam in only a few more minutes.

She hadn't seen him since saying goodbye to him at Janey's place on Saturday. She sighed longingly. Why did holidays always seem to go too fast? She wondered how little David was coping even though she had only spoken to Janey yesterday when she had finally arrived home.

Looking down at what she was writing, to her embarassment Penny realised that she had written the name Sam instead of the patient's name, which was Robert. Groaning, she reached into the drawer for the liquid paper and quickly covered her mistake. She bent her head to concentrate fully on her work.

'Ooh, that man!' Sister walked into the nurses station and threw her pen onto the desk.

'Mr Smithers?' Penny asked with a grin.

'How did you guess?'

'What's the problem? Maybe I can help,' Penny

offered as the sister sat down next to her.

'He's driving me mad. Anyone would think he's just sat his Fellowship and is an expert on hip replacements. Especially how to nurse them.'

Penny nodded. 'I know what you mean. I fully expected him to wake up in the middle of his operation to check that I was doing it correctly—but we should be sympathetic.' She shook her head sadly. 'Patients with Munchausen's syndrome can't help themselves.'

'I know,' the sister grumbled, 'but how much longer is he going to be in? I can't wait for him to be discharged.'

Penny reached over for Mr Smithers's notes. 'Let's see, probably another two to three weeks at the least. I guess it all depends on what other complications arise. I know he's probably buzzing you every ten minutes.'

'Try every five minutes. I'm tempted to disconnect the annoying thing,' Sister interjected.

'But,' Penny continued, 'he's still our responsibility. Maybe I can have a word with the Prof and get Mr Smithers transferred to the rehabilitation hospital sooner.'

'Oh, could you?' Sister's face lit up with delight.

'I can't make any promises and the Prof would have the final say but I'll try.'

'And exactly what are you going to try, Dr Hatfield?' Sam's voice spoke from behind her. It was amazing how the sound of his voice reverberated throughout her entire body, causing her to shiver.

CHAPTER SIX

'COLD, Penny?' he whispered as he walked passed, coming to stand between herself and the sister, a wry grin on his face.

'Professor. . .' Sister unknowingly came to Penny's rescue '. . .we were discussing Mr Smithers in room two. Dr Hatfield has a proposition for you.'

'Does she now?' He turned to face Penny, his back to the sister. Digging his hands deep into his pockets, he waited, his eyes conveying underlying messages to her. 'I'm waiting, Dr Hatfield.' His grin broadened and Penny grew mad at his teasing.

She calmly told him her idea for transferring Mr Smithers sooner rather than later. Sister interjected with comments of her own and the problems it was causing amongst her staff.

'I'll monitor the situation over the next few days and let you know, Sister.' His tone brooked no argument but the smile on the sister's face confirmed that Penny had been correct in approaching him.

'Right. I believe the next order of business was Mrs Brooker and her husband. Has he left the premises?'

'Yes. Carol's still with her and will be able to provide more details but the allegations that Mrs Brooker made to me are serious enough to contact the police immediately.'

'I'll arrange to meet with the police and hospital security but you'll need to be there as well.' He picked up an internal phone and spoke with his secretary. Sister had gone to attend to one of the patients, leaving Penny and Sam alone in the nurses' station.

Penny couldn't take her eyes off him as he fired off brisk commands to his secretary. He had an aura of authority about him that no one dared challenge. He was strong, confident and powerful. She took a step closer and breathed in his musky, male scent. She closed her eyes momentarily, remembering the feel of him against her body.

'Are you all right, Pen?' he asked quietly. Her eyes snapped open immediately to find he had replaced the receiver and was studying her with the desire she knew was mirrored in her own eyes.

Not trusting herself to speak, she nodded, licking her dry lips. Sister re-entered the nurses' station, causing the other two occupants to move quickly and put some distance between them.

'The police should be here in half an hour or so. I'll have you paged when they arrive, Dr Hatfield. If Carol is free at that time then I suggest she accompany you.' His tone was brisk and efficient.

She now knew that his tone was a cover-up as his eyes still spoke of their desire. Or so she hoped.

The next patient she needed to see was Mr Wilson. He'd been discharged from the intensive care unit while she had been on holidays and was now back in his old room on the ward. She knocked and then opened his door. His wife was sitting in a chair next to the bed, knitting.

'Hello. How are you feeling today?' Penny walked to the base of the bed and collected his chart.

'I'm doing just fine, Dr Hatfield. It's great to have you back.' Mr Wilson, although still in the uncomfortable skin traction, beamed at her from ear to ear.

'Did you have a good holiday?' Mrs Wilson asked, not missing a stitch on her knitting.

'Wonderful. Just wish it could have lasted longer.'
Penny glanced down at his chart and asked a few more
questions about his health. The sister had asked him
the same questions not half an hour before but Penny
still wanted to check for herself.

'Where did you go? Somewhere exotic?' Mrs
Wilson grinned at Penny.

'If you call Little River in Victoria exotic, then yes.'

'Country girl at heart, are you?' Mr Wilson chuckled.

'Within twenty minutes of arriving I was sitting on a
beautiful gelding, whisking the cobwebs away,' Penny
laughed. 'One of my dearest friends lives there and it
was great to see her and her family again.'

'Has she got any children?' Mrs Wilson asked
casually.

'Yes. She has lovely twin daughters, aged eight, and
while I was there she had a baby boy.' Penny's eyes
misted temporarily with nostalgia as she remembered
Janey holding David tightly.

'Well, I'll be,' Mrs Wilson gasped as she put her
knitting down. 'Professor Chadwick was away last
week and he stayed with friends who had twin daughters and had a baby boy.'

Penny froze. Sam had been here and told the Wilsons
about his holiday. Maybe they should have discussed
what they were going to tell people before they'd
returned. What if the rest of their colleagues found out
about the time they had spent together? She'd be the
one who got teased, not him. She could just imagine
the look on Derek's face if he found out. He'd be so
smug and would never let her live it down.

Mr Wilson chuckled again and waggled a finger at
his wife in reprimand.

'Don't take any notice of her. She's just teasing you.
Professor Chadwick stopped in here last night on his

way home from the airport. He told us about the coincidence of your mutual friends and how you both brought that little chap into the world. He was full of high praise for his Dr Hatfield.'

'I'm not his. . .' Penny's pager sounded and she looked at the number. It was Sam's extension. The police must have arrived.

She felt more at ease now that Mr Wilson had explained what had happened.

'Well, I'd better go. I'll be back to check on you this evening but if you need me have me paged.' She stopped just before she opened the door and turned to look at Mrs Wilson.

'If you ever pull a stunt like that again—' Penny's grin belied the fierceness of her words '—I'll hand your husband's case over to someone else. Do you have any idea how the hospital grapevine thrives on that kind of news?'

Mrs Wilson giggled again and nodded. 'You're just like our Debbie. I said it to her and I'll say it to you. Don't fight the attraction. Love always gets its victim in the end.'

Penny hid her emotions behind her laughter as she left the Wilsons in peace. Was this love she felt for Sam or was it just an attraction? How could she tell what the difference was? She remembered asking her mother when she was still in high school exactly how you knew you were in love. Her mother had chuckled to herself and told her, 'If you have to ask, then you're not in love.'

Penny arrived at Sam's office, knocked and went in. She'd expected to find the room full of police officers and security people but there was only Sam. He was standing at the window, looking out to the street below. She stopped just inside the door, unsure whether he had heard her knock. Maybe she should have waited for him to acknowledge her knock before she had entered?

He turned to look at her then motioned for her to join him. She stood beside him and followed his gaze down to the street. There were about twenty pink flamingos standing on the front lawn of the hospital grounds. It took a second to realise that they were wooden cut-outs and not the real thing.

There was a large white noticeboard in the centre which read HAPPY 40TH BIRTHDAY, JUDY. Penny had no idea who Judy was but thought the flamingos a novel idea. She turned to face Sam, smiling. He smiled back and for a moment nothing else in the world existed except the two of them.

Penny could feel her heartbeat pound out loud and strong as Sam's eyes travelled the length of her body. She was wearing her usual shorts and shirt with her white coat slung over the top.

'I really liked you in that skirt you wore the other week,' he murmured, his breath fanning her ear.

'I know,' she smiled back. 'Why do you think I wore it?'

They both stood there, feeling the tension build, and as Sam's head began its now-familiar descent toward her lips they were interrupted by the intercom on Sam's desk.

'Professor Chadwick, the police officers have arrived.'

Sam strode to his desk and punched the button on the intercom.

'Send them in. Would you mind making refreshments?'

'I'll see to it, Professor.'

A second later the door was opened and two uniformed police officers entered. Sam motioned for them to take a seat.

'Sergeant Metcalfe and Senior Sergeant Cobb,' Sergeant Metcalfe introduced herself and her tall, male partner. There was another knock at the door and Carol entered, along with Gus—a member of the hospital security staff.

The meeting lasted just over two hours and Penny was starving by the time they came out. Both she and Sam were due in Theatre that afternoon and she was determined to get something to eat.

She was ushered out of Sam's office by Carol who wanted to discuss a few confidential aspects of Maureen Brooker's treatment. Penny had no alternative but to go with her. She had wanted to stay with Sam and perhaps even have lunch with him.

She stamped out her feelings of annoyance for Carol and listened attentively to what she had to say. After another half-hour tucked away in Carol's excuse for an office Penny's stomach did all of the talking for her.

'I'm sorry, Carol, but I really do need to get something to eat. I'm due in Theatre in another half-hour and need to feed my stomach something before its groaning can embarrass me further,' she laughed and Carol let her go.

She met Derek in the cafeteria and sat with him while she ate her salad roll.

'Could you get me a cup of coffee, please, Derek?' she pleaded as she continued to chew on her roll.

'Only if you promise to have dinner with me tonight.' He rose from the table to get the coffee. Penny wondered which girlfriend he was having trouble with now. She asked as much when he returned.

'It's Cindy-Lou again,' he confessed sheepishly. 'She's going out tonight with her brother who's in town for the evening. She's told me the restaurant that they're going to but I told her that I had to work. If you and I go to the same restaurant then she'll get the hint and dump me.'

Penny shook her head sadly at her friend. 'Why don't you just break it off instead of making excuses and playing charades? Just tell her that you feel no magic and it would be better for all concerned if you didn't see each other again.'

'I couldn't do that. She might get hurt.'

Penny knew she was getting nowhere so she tried another track.

'What if the person she's going out with tonight isn't really her brother? What if she's trying to give *you* a hint, hoping that you'll dump her? Or what if she sees us together and decides that you are worth fighting for? I'm certainly not going to fight another woman for you.' Penny chuckled as she swallowed the last of her drink. 'Thanks for the coffee, old friend, but I must run to Theatre.'

'So what time should I pick you up?' Derek said hurriedly as she pushed her chair back and stood.

'Don't bother.' Sam's voice came from behind Penny. 'She'll be in Theatre until late.'

Penny turned, a startled look on her face. Where had he sprung from and how much of their conversation had he heard? Although she was terribly attracted to Sam and could feel her desire for him growing more and more with each passing day there was no way she was going to let him speak for her. Especially in matters that didn't concern him. She turned back to Derek, whose face was now as white as a ghost's.

'Before the professor rudely interrupted us, Derek, I was going to suggest that you take my advice and call Cindy-Lou. Tell her the truth.' She gave him a wry

grin. 'Besides we probably will be delayed in Theatre.'
Penny snapped her fingers as a thought occurred to her.
'If the worst comes to the worst you could always join
us in Theatre. The more the merrier, right, Sam?' Penny
grinned at them both before leaving the cafeteria.

Sam was hot on her heels and caught up with her in
the long corridor that led to the theatre block.

'Just what was that all about?' He placed a hand on
her arm to stop her progress. 'I've asked you to call
me Professor around the rest of the staff.'

'For heaven's sake, Sam. It was only Derek.' Penny
turned and continued on her way. Sam was silent as
they walked through the theatre block toward the
changing-rooms. Females on the right and Males on
the left. He turned in the small, deserted corridor to
face her.

' "Only Derek",' he mimicked. 'It's only Derek that
hospital gossip says you're having an affair with.'

'And you believe hospital gossip?' she asked
incredulously. 'Well, let me tell you, my darling
Professor, that Derek is my friend. That's all. No more,
no less. You, on the other hand. . .' she leaned closer
to him, dropping her voice to an angry whisper '. . .are
more to me than just a friend. We've both admitted
that the attraction's there so, for heaven's sake, let's
do something about it.'

She planted a kiss firmly on his unsuspecting lips
before turning and entering the female changing-
rooms.

The theatre list went well although, as predicted, they
finished late. It was almost seven-thirty when Penny
had changed out of her theatre blues.

Sam had not said one word to her concerning her
outburst before entering the changing-rooms. Not that

she had expected him to in front of the theatre staff.
They had worked well, as the rest of the theatre staff
were coming to expect, and managed to get through a
right total hip replacement, an arthroscopic synovec-
tomy and three knee arthroscopies.

She walked out of the hospital and was on her way
to her car when she heard someone calling her name.
Déjà vu, she thought as Sam jogged up to her side.
This time he was slightly more dishevelled than he had
been two weeks ago. His shirt was unbuttoned from
the top with his tie slung around his neck.

'How do you manage to change so quickly?' He
gave her a lopsided grin which he obviously thought
would melt her heart. It did but she wasn't going to let
him know that. She was still partly angry with him for
believing hospital gossip. Did he honestly think that
she would be having an affair with Derek while she
accepted his passes and mild love-making?

'I'd like to apologise,' he began, when he realised
she wasn't going to be teased from her black mood.
'You were right. I don't usually listen to hospital gossip
and I'm sorry if I've upset you.'

Penny still remained silent, unsure of his sincerity.

'I'd like to make it up to you—if you'll let me.'

'How?' Her voice was husky and she chided herself
for letting his boyish charm break through her resolve.

'Your rain-check for the movies. I still haven't seen
the new Arnold Schwarzenegger movie.' He grinned
from ear to ear, thoroughly pleased with himself.

'Dinner first, with popcorn during the movie,' she
stated her price and Sam held out a hand for them to
shake on the deal.

'Done. Where would the lady care to dine?'

Penny thought for a moment. 'Somewhere Italian.
You choose. I'd really like to go home and change first.

Can I meet you at the restaurant in an hour?'

'I'll pick you up,' he said, his voice now as husky as hers had been moments ago. He didn't try to kiss her but the look he gave her before he turned and strode away was one that set her entire body blazing.

Penny hurried home to quickly shower and change. Knowing that Sam liked her in a skirt, she dug out a cool cotton skirt which she matched with a sleeveless top. She was ready when Sam came to the door precisely an hour after they had parted. He'd changed into casual trousers and shirt, his thick, black hair still slightly damp.

The movie started at nine-thirty, giving them just under an hour to eat. Sam helped Penny into his blue Jaguar XJ6 and started driving back toward the city. She was too concerned with controlling her rising emotions to realise for a while that Sam wasn't making any attempt to park the car and was instead driving straight through the city.

'Where are we going?' she finally asked as he turned into a darkened street, lit by the occasional street light.

'My place.' His voice held deep promises and Penny wondered whether they'd ever make it to the movies.

'You run an Italian restaurant from your house?' she said in an attempt to lighten the atmosphere. He turned into a driveway and shut the engine off. Sensor lights came on automatically and Penny received her first glimpse of the sandstone, two-storey home.

He chuckled. 'It seems like it some days. I've been considering investing in Antonio's restaurant. I eat there often enough.'

'So, you have a fetish for pasta?' she joked in her best mafia voice. They both laughed and Penny felt more relaxed. Sam came around to help her out of the car.

'I used to eat at Antonio's three, maybe four, times a week. Now that I've taken up the Chair at the university and my workload has consequently doubled, Antonio graciously delivers the food to my home on my request. If he didn't I probably wouldn't eat.' He unlocked the front door and flicked a switch.

'So, what delights have you ordered for us tonight?' Penny asked as she walked into the entrance-way.

So this was Sam's place. It was everything she had dreamed of. This was her kind of house.

The floors were stained wood panels with large Persian rugs in the main living rooms of the house. She walked into the lounge room, openly admiring the many classical prints hung around the walls. There were books and photographs everywhere, giving the room a very lived in atmosphere.

'Sam. Your home is. . .' she searched for the correct word '. . .divine. How long have you lived here?' Unable to stop herself, Penny wandered around the room, glancing at the photographs. There were many pictures of a younger Sam with his parents. On holiday—in the back yard with the dogs—his graduation day.

'Since I was seven. When my parents died four years ago I moved back to the only real home I'd ever known.'

'I'm sorry. I didn't mean to pry.' Penny quickly sat down on the sofa.

'It's all right.' He came to sit next to her and gently took one of her hands in his. 'I want you to know.' His voice was soft and sweet and Penny closed her eyes for a moment in the hope of remembering this night for ever.

'My father died of a heart attack and my mother died one week after him. They couldn't bear to be parted.

They were both in their eighties as they'd had me quite late in their lives. We were all good friends and I have only the fondest memories of them.'

Silence reigned in the room, except for the soft ticking of the grandfather clock. Penny couldn't break the contact of his eyes and felt herself being drawn closer to him. Their lips were barely touching when the loud peal of the doorbell rang out through the still house.

Sam stood and cleared his throat. 'That will be Antonio.' He went to the door to receive their food and Penny could hear the deep, muffled voices as the two men talked. The aroma was beginning to invade the house and Penny's stomach began to make loud grumbling noises. Why did she have to have one of those embarrassing stomachs? Sam returned, smiling, laden with food which he deposited on the coffee-table.

'Would you care to adjourn to the dining-room?'

Penny shook her head. 'I'd much rather sit on the floor and eat in here, if you don't mind. This room is so comfortable.'

Sam grinned and nodded. 'I'll fetch the glasses and wine.'

Penny began to unload the food, making herself comfortable on a large cushion. Sam set the glasses down and began to pour the wine as Penny exclaimed exultantly, '*Fettuccine marinara*. That's my favourite pasta dish.'

'I know,' came his deep voice as he sat down on another large cushion opposite her. At Penny's frown he elaborated. 'Janey and I had an in-depth discussion about your likes and dislikes after you'd left. She also explained why she still owes you money.'

Penny flushed scarlet and Sam chuckled. 'Some friend she is,' she joked, trying to cover her annoyance with Janey. Why did the woman have to persistently match her up? She'd have some strong words to say to her friend the next time they spoke.

They ate in a companionable silence, savouring the delightful cuisine. With feigned agony Penny forked the final mouthful of her delicious dinner into her mouth.

'That was wonderful but I'm completely full. You must pass on my heartfelt appreciation to Antonio.' Penny leaned back against the sofa, watching Sam clear away the debris. He sat down next to her, his arm slung casually around her shoulders.

'Did you really mean what you said outside the changing-rooms?' he asked gently and Penny turned to look at him.

'That Derek is my friend? Yes, of course I meant it.' She deliberately misunderstood him and he shook his head slightly.

'You know what I mean, Pen. Do you honestly think that we should do something about the attraction between us?' He raised his hand to brush his fingers through her hair. 'You didn't just say that in the heat of the moment?'

'If I hadn't meant it I wouldn't have said it and why are you giving me an opportunity to back out?' Penny asked, her voice barely audible. Sam's caress was doing disastrous things to her heartbeat. She felt her mouth go dry as his head dipped toward hers. Nervously she licked her lips, causing a groan to escape from Sam seconds before his lips came down on hers. She felt the ground disappear from beneath her and a floating sensation engulf her as his mouth began its onslaught.

At first his lips were soft and gentle, nibbling at hers, tasting them. Her arms crept up and Penny marvelled at his firm body as her fingers felt their way along his muscled torso.

She wanted to feel the *real* him, without the obstacles that clothing provided. As her fingers began fumbling with the buttons on his shirt, Sam groaned again before his kiss became more fierce and intent. He cradled her face in his hands, his tongue plundering the depths of her mouth.

Penny gently tugged his shirt from the waistband of his trousers. Suffering more from impatience now rather than uncertainty, she undid the last few buttons before pushing the fabric from his body and sending her flattened palms across the contours of his chest.

'Oh, Pen,' Sam gasped as he covered her face and neck with small butterfly kisses. Pausing at her ear, he nibbled the lobe.

'I've wanted you since the moment I laid eyes on you in that theatre. Your deep brown eyes spoke directly to my soul and I've felt bereft ever since.' His breath fanned out across her neck and Penny shivered slightly.

'I know.' She dipped her head to kiss his neck. 'I felt it too,' was all she could say as Sam's mouth claimed hers once more, demanding and eliciting a response.

He ran a hand over first one breast and then the other before reaching down to mimic her own actions and free her top from the band of her skirt. Her top was up and over her head in a matter of seconds.

'You're so beautiful,' he whispered. As she watched his eyes hungrily drank in the sight of her semi-naked body. His gaze was as soft as a caress, making her head light and giddy with desire.

Slowly Penny felt his warm hands run over her satiny skin before reaching around to unhook her bra. Together they removed the flimsy lace article before he urged her gently backwards, her back making contact with the softness of the Persian rug beneath her.

She observed Sam through dreamy eyes as he lay on his side, facing her. One hand supported his neck, while the other wrought havoc with her emotions as he trailed his fingers across her chest.

As though in a daze Penny watched his head descend toward the area his fingers had just left. She closed her eyes, waiting, anticipating the softness of his mouth as it closed around the rosy peak of her breast. At the moment of contact a searing heat flooded Penny's entire body, ending in a nerve-shattering explosion of ecstasy. Sam lifted his head, their eyes meeting through the passion-filled daze that had captured them both.

'You're so exquisitely beautiful,' he murmured again as his head began its agonisingly slow descent to claim her lips once again.

The grandeur of the moment swept Penny up on a wave of desire. She experienced previously unknown sensations: tingling in her fingertips; the sounds of distant bells ringing.

A chill swept over her and she shivered involuntarily. It took a few seconds to realise that Sam wasn't by her side any more but was instead striding angrily across the room to quieten the persistent ringing of the telephone.

Penny sat upright and quickly donned her clothing. Regardless of who the phone call was from, the atmosphere had definitely been broken. As a doctor she knew all too well that phone calls must be answered but she wished that just this once they could have ignored it.

'The leg is fine, Mrs Gregory.' Penny pulled the X-rays off the viewer and turned to face her patient. 'We'll put you in a support splint for another two weeks just to make sure that the bone doesn't re-fracture. Make sure you follow my advice to the letter this time and let your husband do the housework,' she scolded humorously and Mrs Gregory nodded.

'I'll see you in another two weeks' time but, again, please have me paged if there are any problems.'

'Excuse me, Dr Hatfield.' Lauren poked her head around the door. 'There's a phone call for you.'

Penny gave Lauren her instructions regarding Mrs Gregory before going into a small consulting-room to answer her call.

'It's just me, Pen, darling.' Her father's chirpy voice came across the line, causing a smile to light Penny's face. 'Mother just wanted me to check that you've not been held up with an emergency. She's making your favourite,' he added in a whisper.

'I've just seen the last patient, Dad.' Penny's eyes flew up to the doorway as Sam entered the room. He shut the door behind him and was obviously wanting to speak to her. She held up a finger, indicating that she would only be a moment.

'I'll be leaving the hospital in another fifteen minutes so tell Mum it'll be OK if she dishes up for sevenish.' Penny paused, laughing at her father's reply. 'That's right.' Her voice feigned indignation. 'Use your daughter as a courier service. Does she want anything else, bread. . .milk?' Penny could feel Sam's eyes travelling hungrily over her body as she concluded her conversation and replaced the receiver.

'I feel like I haven't seen you in days,' he said softly, 'when in reality it's been less than twenty-four hours.'

They kept their distance with the desk safely between them but their expressions spoke volumes. Who knew when anyone might walk in?

'I was going to ask you out tonight but I gather you've already made plans.'

Penny nodded. 'Sorry. I have a meal with my parents

once a week and I would break it except that my mother's already started her preparations.' It was on the tip of her tongue to invite him along but knew that she needed more time alone to come to terms with the direction of their relationship.

'Never mind,' he said as though he could read her mind. 'I'll see you tomorrow morning at the X-ray meeting.' He reached out for her hand and held it tenderly in his. 'Dream about me,' he whispered, before turning and walking out the door.

True to her word, Penny was on the road heading toward her parents' home exactly fifteen minutes later. Once she'd negotiated her car through the peak-hour traffic, she put on some melancholy music that seemed to reflect her mood.

She could be out with Sam at that moment—sharing his sweet company, laughing together and discussing their work without the fear of boring the other person.

She remembered the look of relief in Sam's eyes, knowing that she understood the medical emergency that had interrupted their passion. Penny had been in that position too many times to count. If she had been paged when out on a date, the person she was with couldn't even begin to understand her dedication to her job. That was one of the main reasons why she had begun to see Derek socially.

Penny had accompanied Sam to the hospital, only to find that she too had been needed. The patient had been a road accident victim with multiple fractures to her right leg and pelvis. Ms Karen Deluth was a twenty-five-year-old, single woman whose car had been hit by another car. The other driver had died on impact. The police suspected that he had fallen asleep at the wheel before crashing headlong into Ms Deluth's car, which had subsequently been crushed like a tin can.

They had finished in Theatre just after two in the morning. Sam had driven her home, neither of them in an amorous mood, but he had still kissed her to distraction before leaving her to get some sleep. She was more than a little confused about her feelings for Sam but knew that she was already beginning to fall hopelessly in love with him.

Her thoughts were still on Sam when she pulled into her parents' driveway ten minutes before seven o'clock, now totally exhausted.

'Hi, Sis,' Eric called to her as she walked through the door. His body was slumped over the sofa, his eyes glued to the television.

'Hi yourself,' Penny grinned back. It was the way they had greeted each other for years and she loved the familiarity of it.

Her mother had indeed made her favourite dish. Beef Wellington with steamed vegetables and home-made strawberry cheesecake for dessert.

'Why do you go to so much trouble, Mum?' Penny asked between mouthfuls of the delicious, mouth-watering dessert.

'Because I know how hard you work, love. I know I was only a nurse and that nursing has changed completely but the medical profession still remains extremely stressful and if you can't come home and enjoy a good home-cooked meal, what can you enjoy?' Ellen sighed as she turned fond eyes toward her husband. 'It always used to relax your father.'

Penny looked from her father and then to her mother, hoping that when she was their age, she would be as much in love with Sam as she was now. In love with Sam? She bent her head and held it in her hands for a moment. It was true! Her subconscious had obviously known it for a while and was now forcing her conscious to acknowledge it. She was in love with Samuel Chadwick.

'So, Pen,' her father's voice cut through her thoughts, 'how's that new professor of yours settling in?'

Penny choked on her mouthful of cheesecake and reached for her drink. Did her father know what was going on between the two of them? As soon as the thought had entered her head, Penny dismissed it. Her father was asking a general question.

'He's fine, Dad.' She took another sip of her drink. 'What's his name again?'

'Chadwick. Samuel Chadwick. Why, was he an ex-intern of yours?' Penny grinned, wondering whether she was going to find out some of Sam's history.

'The name doesn't ring a bell but, then again, I couldn't remember one intern from the next.' Her father stood from his chair and turned to her. 'I was looking through some of the old medical school end-of-year books today. Would you care to join me for a peek at the past?'

Penny nodded and quickly finished her dessert. She remembered flicking through them years ago and hadn't given them a second thought. Sam had told her that he'd lived most of his life in an inner city suburb, which could mean that he trained at the medical school attached to their hospital.

An hour later she found her answer. A picture of a very much younger looking Sam in a group photograph of medical students. They all had their arms around each other's shoulders, grinning at the camera as though the world was their oyster.

She scanned the words below, putting names with the faces of his friends. The text was formal and there were a few 'Mrs' amongst the women, the men all labelled as 'Mr'.

There was a young woman standing next to Sam. Her face had turned to look at him instead of the camera, her long, blonde hair pulled carelessly back in a ponytail. She had a smile of adoration on her face and Penny had a sudden urge to know her name.

She read the name and then immediately felt ill. The woman's name was Mrs Mary Chadwick. Sam was married.

CHAPTER SEVEN

PENNY slammed the year-book closed as though abruptly finishing a part of her life. Jumping to her feet, she raced for the bathroom, one hand clamped over her mouth.

She brought up the contents of her stomach then spent the next half-hour convincing her family that she was all right.

'I want you to stay here tonight,' her mother insisted.

'I can't. I have meetings and Theatre tomorrow.'

'The hospital can run efficiently without you, dear,' Ellen preached. Penny had heard her use the same argument against her father countless times.

She almost capitulated to her mother's idea. Maybe she could stay here. That way, she wouldn't have to face Sam tomorrow.

Not tomorrow but the next day, she reasoned with herself. It was inevitable that she would see him again unless she suddenly wanted to change careers.

'I appreciate your concern, Mum, but I'll be fine. It's probably a twenty-four-hour bug I've picked up.'

Saying goodbye to her family, she started the drive home. The radio transmitted another love song and Penny angrily switched it off.

How dared he do this to her, especially when she had only just realised that she was in love with him? She had trusted him with her very being and this was what he had done to her. Well, she told herself sternly, she would never let this happen again. All men were creeps and, as far as she was concerned, Samuel Chadwick was their leader.

Why had he deceived her? How many other women had he toyed with until it was too late? Until they, too, had fallen hopelessly and irresponsibly in love with him?

Sam had cunningly drawn her out of her comfort zone, using himself as her life line, before severing the rope, sending her plummeting into the depths of despair.

Penny pulled the car onto the side of the road and wept. 'How could he?' she asked out loud. 'I've been waiting twenty-nine years for my perfect man to come along and when he finally does he turns out to be false.' She blew her nose fiercely. 'What's wrong with me? Why did this have to happen to me?'

She waited for a long moment but no answer came. Taking a deep breath, she started the engine and continued on her drive home.

Wearily, Penny pulled into the driveway. She unlocked the front door, dumping her bag on the floor before going to her bedroom. Her eyes were red and puffy from crying. She walked over to her bedside drawer and extracted a clean handkerchief, just in case. The words kept repeating themselves over and over in her head. Sam was a married man.

Sighing heavily, she performed the rituals of teeth-brushing and changing for bed. She had a headache from the emotional roller-coaster and took an analgesic to combat it.

Waking just after six o'clock, Penny contemplated staying in bed all day. It was tempting to hide from reality and wallow in self-pity but she knew that the moment she called in sick Sam would probably be wanting to know why she wasn't at work.

Sam. Just the thought of him hurt. She hoped that the sight of him wouldn't reopen the floodgates.

She reluctantly left her bed and began to shower. The only place she had left to go—the place where she knew she was needed and important—was the hospital. Work was her comfort zone. Work was familiar. The easiest thing to do was to withdraw from Sam.

Why hadn't he mentioned his wife? Where was she? There was certainly no feminine presence in his home. There weren't even any photographs, other than those of him and his parents.

But, she thought as she vigorously shampooed her hair, even if he was separated from his wife why hadn't he mentioned her? No. She could not forgive him. Even more to the point, could she forgive herself?

She had been more than ready to accept him at face value. True, she hadn't been able to cope with his personality-switching at first but after the glorious week they had spent with Janey and Craig Penny had been more than willing to participate in his passionate embraces.

Switching off the taps, she towelled herself dry before returning to her room to dress. Just the thought of how close she had come to surrendering her body to him was enough to make her tremble. He had made her feel so wonderful. He was truly a masterful lover but, in the light of her discovery, Penny knew that she would never experience the complete extent of his qualifications in that department.

Dressed only in her underwear, Penny felt her eyes begin to mist over again with tears. They poured down her cheeks to splash unheard on her carpeted floor. She let her knees buckle beneath her, landing gently on the bed. Just as she had as a child, Penny buried her head deep in the pillow and began to sob her heart out.

Half an hour later she felt much better and returned to the bathroom to wash her face and hands. She now knew that work was going to be her only salvation against heartbreak.

She would just have to cut herself off from all emotion. It was the only way she could freeze Sam out of her life. Hopefully he'd take the hint sooner rather than later and once he did Penny knew that he would treat her with as much indifference as she wanted to feel for him.

'There is a visible step on the joint surface in the X-rays of the knee taken at forty and sixty degrees of flexion. . .' Dr Markum was saying as Penny sneaked in the back door of the meeting room. She had purposely delayed her arrival, hiding in the ladies toilets in an effort to avoid Sam.

'Where'd you get to?' Derek leaned across and whispered in her ear as she sat down next to him. She shook her head in answer and focussed her attention on Dr Markum's report.

Outwardly she was composed but inwardly she was shaking like a leaf. Her eyes scanned the room for Sam. He was sitting in the front row, his body turned slightly in the chair to show off his profile. She studied him for a few minutes but quickly turned her eyes back to Dr Markum as she felt fresh tears begin to build.

Her training as a doctor had taught her to detach herself from situations. To remain calm, cool and efficient no matter what the cost. If she had allowed herself to think of patients as live human beings, whose lives she literally held in her hands whilst operating, then she would have cracked under the pressure a long time ago.

She would need to draw on every ounce of detachment she could muster to see herself through this situation with Sam. She needed to be strong, not swayed by his good looks and charm. She swallowed the lump in her throat and straightened her shoulders.

'Penny?' Derek whispered beside her and she realised that she had been day-dreaming. She refocussed her attention to realise that everyone was looking at her. All thirty pairs of eyes were on her. She had obviously been asked a question and for the life of her she didn't know what it was. Her eyes briefly flicked to Sam's but his expression was neutral.

She cleared her throat and as she opened her mouth to speak a beeping sound pierced the stillness in the room. Thirty-one pairs of eyes glanced down at their pagers before Penny, blessedly, realised that it was hers.

Thankful that she was at the back of the room, she quickly stood and all but ran out of the room. She knew that it was extremely unprofessional of her to just up and depart. Not to mention her lack of attention to Dr Markum's report. Hopefully, the speed of her exit would cause her colleagues to explain her behaviour as preoccupation with a troubling case.

Penny finally reached the registrar's office and sank down into a chair. She leant on the table and buried her head in her hands. Get a grip, Hatfield, she instructed herself sharply. Her pager sounded again and she quickly rang the number.

It was the theatre sister, double-checking the instruments for their afternoon operating list. It was ten minutes later that Penny replaced the receiver. She slumped back in the chair, letting her hands hang down limply toward the floor as she shut her eyes.

This was undoubtedly the worst day of her life. She

heard the door open and close. Slowly she opened her eyes. Sam was standing there, immaculate in his suit. Now the worst day of her life was going to get decidedly worse.

'Pen, are you all right?' He came over to her, quickly grasping one of her hands. His touch burnt and Penny quickly withdrew from the touch.

'Don't call me that,' she said quietly. Standing up, she pushed the chair under the table before taking a few steps back, putting some much needed distance between them.

Sam stood, a puzzled frown creasing his forehead. He took a step toward her and she took another step back, coming into contact with the bench.

'Penny. What on earth is the matter? Are you feeling ill?' His tone was caring and Penny felt herself weaken. He took another step closer, then another. He was within touching distance and Penny could feel her body begin to betray her, swaying toward his.

He reached out a hand before touching her forehead. 'You feel rather hot to me.' His hand slid down to rest at the side of her neck. He looked at his watch while he counted the beats.

'Your pulse is high, too. I think you should go home and rest.' His hand caressed her cheek and Penny felt her knees weaken. She leant against his chest, breathing in deeply the scent of his aftershave. She loved him so much that it really was making her sick.

Then she remembered his wife. She probably loved him too. The memory was enough to give her the strength to push away from him. She jammed her hands into the pockets of her white coat.

'I'm fine, thank you, Professor. Now, if you'll excuse me.' She pushed past him.

'Will you tell me what on earth is going on?' His

voice cut through the air and pierced her heart.

'I'm going up to Theatre to check on the instruments for this afternoon's theatre, Professor,' she said, her voice a little shaky.

'Will you stop with the "Professor"?' he demanded, covering the distance between them with a few angry strides. 'What's going on, Penny?' He grabbed her shoulders and almost shook her.

Penny took a deep breath. Here was the moment of truth.

'I can't see you any more. It was a mistake.' The words tumbled out on top of each other. Penny bent her head, hoping that Sam wouldn't see the tears that were gathering there.

'What?' he bellowed, then his eyes narrowed as he lifted her chin so that their eyes could meet. 'What happened to you last night that has caused you to have such a change of heart?'

'Nothing,' Penny denied, a little too quickly.

'You're lying.' He was quiet for a moment before the hands on her shoulders released their grip and began rubbing up and down. 'Trust me, Penny. Tell me what's wrong.' He gathered her close and held her tight. She could feel herself succumbing to his charms once again.

Slowly he bent his head to claim her lips, the touch sending a liquid fire through her body. It felt so right to be held by Sam, to be kissed by Sam. Why did it have to be so wrong?

Penny broke free and looked into the blue depths of his eyes.

'I'm sorry, Sam,' she whispered. 'I can't.' A single tear ran down her cheek before she turned and fled from the room.

*　　*　　*

The theatre staff were ready and waiting with the patient prepped and on the table. Penny was at the sink, still scrubbing. They were all waiting for Sam. The scout nurse had phoned through ten minutes ago and had been informed by his secretary that he had already left.

They had two total knee replacements and three arthroscopies to get through that afternoon. Personally, Penny just wanted to get this day over and done with. She had locked herself into a toilet cubicle down in the basement of the hospital until her tears had dried and her face had lost its puffy redness.

'If you scrub any harder, Dr Hatfield, you'll be admitted as a candidate for skin grafts.' Sam had appeared beside her, his voice as hard as nails. Penny watched as he flicked the taps on, the water pumping out of them vigorously.

Coming to her senses, she turned off her taps with her elbows before turning to be gowned and gloved. His disposition didn't appear to be at its best and she knew that the theatre list was going to be a disaster.

They were halfway through the second knee replacement when the telephone rang, startling the instrument nurse who was deep in concentration. She jumped in shock, the action upsetting the instrument trolley, which crashed to the floor with a deafening clatter.

'Of all the incompetence,' Sam roared, turning his anger to the nurse in question. 'Get out of my theatre. Someone clear up this mess and someone else answer the phone,' he demanded, sending the remaining occupants of the theatre into action.

Sam stood back from the table, hands up-held while his eyes bored into Penny's. She stood on the other side of the table and was certain that if the patient hadn't been between them Sam would have fixed his bloodied hands around her small neck and throttled her.

Penny held his gaze, knowing that she was the one who had put him in this foul mood.

'Stop taking your anger out on everyone else, Sam,' she said quietly, knowing that the rest of the staff were too busy cleaning up to overhear her words. 'It's me you're angry with.'

'What do you suggest I do to you, then?' His tone was clipped and Penny was sure that his lips were compressed into a thin line beneath his mask.

'Just stop taking it out on everyone else.' The instruments had been collected from the floor and a new sterilised tray was being placed beside Sam. 'Three nurses have already left here in tears and the rest of the staff are treading on eggshells in case you decide to turn your foul temper on one of them. Please, let's get this list over and done with,' she implored and he nodded slightly.

'Let's continue,' he announced to the theatre, his tone still brisk.

The theatre remained silent except for clipped instructions from Sam. Penny could feel the relief in the room when they finally completed the knee replacement without further confrontation or mistakes.

Penny had just finished de-gowning when Sam came and stood beside her. She felt a tingle of apprehension run down her spine. His face was void of emotion, his eyes cold.

'My secretary has called through. She couldn't get me out of the Heads of Department meeting. Apparently they need me for a vote so I must attend. You finish off the list. No doubt it will be to the theatre staff's delight.' He turned sharply and walked toward the changing-rooms.

Penny released her breath, unaware that she had been

holding it. She sank down into the closest chair and put her head between her legs. It felt as though her heart was breaking in two and she hoped that it would soon begin to heal. Would it ever get any easier to see Sam? She hoped so.

'Dr Hatfield.' A theatre sister came and sat beside her. 'Are you all right?'

Penny raised her head. 'I'm fine. Professor Chadwick has had to leave to attend an important meeting so I'll finish off the list.' Penny almost laughed at the relief that crossed the other woman's face.

'Right, Dr Hatfield. I'll inform the rest of the staff and get the next patient organised. Why don't you have a cup of tea? I'll call you in the tea-room when we're ready.'

Penny nodded and made her way to the tea-room. She had just finished making her tea when Derek walked into the room and shut the door.

'I was hoping I'd catch you between cases. Are you all right?' Derek came over to her and placed a hand on her forehead. Penny almost laughed aloud. He was the third person in one day to ask that question. She must really look awful.

'I'm fine. I'm just a little tired, that's all.' She took her cup and sat down. Derek came and sat beside her.

'I hear the Prof's been on the rampage again.'

'Yeah. How'd you hear so quickly?' Penny hoped that her face had remained neutral at the mention of Sam.

'The moment I stepped inside the door at Theatre Reception, I was told. The Prof is big news, especially when he's mad. You're close to him, Penny. Can't you sweet-talk him out of his moods?'

Penny was about to refute his statement and to say that she wasn't close to Sam but Derek continued,

'Don't deny it. I've been watching you two closely and I'm positive there is something romantic between you.'

'There was,' Penny sighed and ran a hand through her curls. 'I'm the reason he was in a bad mood. I've called it off.'

'Why? You two were perfect for each other. Even I could see that.'

'Derek, I'd rather not discuss it.'

'Why not? I'm one of your closest friends, Penny. Tell me what's wrong. Why won't it work? You can't say that he doesn't care for you. He practically jumped down my throat every time I so much as looked at you. The guy was jealous.' Derek placed an arm around her shoulders and gave a little squeeze. 'Tell Uncle Derek what the problem is. Maybe I can help?'

'He's married, Derek,' she said quietly as she turned to look at her friend, unable to keep the tears from her eyes.

The phone rang and Penny quickly snatched it up, thankful to have something to occupy her mind.

'I'm on my way,' she said before replacing the receiver. 'I've got to go. Sam's left to attend a meeting so at least I can finish the list in peace.' She stood and turned to look at Derek. Slowly he got to his feet before pulling her into his arms for a hug. Penny felt reassured by his friendliness.

'I'd better go. I'll see you tomorrow.' She pulled away and headed for the door.

'Would you like to have dinner tonight? Not to chase away any old girlfriends,' he grinned but Penny shook her head.

'I don't think I'd be very good company. Maybe another night. Thanks.' She opened the door and made her way to Theatre. She scrubbed and entered the theatre, reading the relief on the staff's faces.

Penny cleared her throat. 'As you all know, Professor Chadwick has been called away. Let's celebrate.' The comment earned her a hearty laugh from her colleagues. Ironically, she didn't feel like laughing at all.

'OK,' she said a bit more seriously. 'Let's get these arthroscopies out of the way so we can all go home.'

'Dr Hatfield, could you please check on Karen Deluth?' The ward sister came over to where Penny was writing up case notes.

'Sure. Has her temperature risen?'

'Yes.'

Penny had been concerned about Karen since she'd done a ward round that morning. She was only two days post-op and hadn't been responding well to treatment with the external fixator that was on her leg. There were no complications with her pelvic fracture, which was a blessing in disguise.

Penny organised for a mobile X-ray to be taken to check on the progress of the fracture. There was no sign of callus formation and she suspected that the fixator was not functioning correctly.

Penny remembered Sam telling her about the new techniques in external fixation that had been presented at the conference. Maybe they could get hold of this new external fixator that was guaranteed not to jam. She'd have to discuss it with him and she wished she didn't have to see him again so soon. For her patient's sake she'd do it.

She phoned his secretary and was told to come up straight away as he had ten minutes to spare before his next meeting. Penny felt herself begin to tremble. She hadn't seen him since he had walked out of theatre yesterday. He may have been out of sight but he had been on her mind constantly.

Penny collected the X-rays and began the walk toward his office, her feet dragging as though she was meeting a firing squad. She tried not to think of the pain she was feeling, nor how she had cried herself to sleep last night only to wake with a severe headache this morning.

She had been dreading seeing him on the ward round in case he had put her through another three-ringed circus but he'd been at a meeting and unable to attend.

She knocked gently on his door and waited. Nothing. She knocked again, a little louder.

'Come in,' he bellowed. She raised a shaky hand to the doorknob and turned it.

'Dr Hatfield. What a surprise.' He didn't sound surprised at all. Penny walked over to his desk where she stood waiting for him to offer her a seat.

'Please sit down. What can I do for you? Or maybe the question I should ask is what *can't* I do for you? You haven't changed your mind again, have you, Penny?'

Penny began to see red. 'Drop the sarcasm, Sam. It doesn't suit you. I haven't come here to talk about our personal lives.'

'That'd be a first,' he bickered.

'I'm worried about Karen Deluth.' Penny ignored his sarcasm. If she could get through this then she could get through anything.

'Just tell me what I've done wrong.' He wasn't listening to her. He stood and walked over to the window. Penny swivelled in her chair to look at him. 'You're attracted to me; I'm attracted to you. We've both admitted this.' He turned to face her, his hands held outward. 'What's the problem?'

She shook her head. 'There's more to it than that, Sam. Now, about Karen Deluth. . .'

'Are you waiting for an admission of undying love?

If you are, you'll be waiting quite a while. Why can't we just go with what we have? A mutual attraction.'

The look in his eyes was almost enough to make Penny capitulate and rush across the room to his open arms. Almost but not quite.

'If you don't know what the problem is then there is definitely no reason to continue with the attraction.' She held her head high, giving an outward appearance of being cool, calm and collected.

'Is it another man? What about the guy you had tucked away in the sister's office the day of Mr Wilson's operation? Is it him?' Sam crossed his arms defensively.

Maybe Derek was right. Sam was jealous but that still didn't give him the right to carry on an affair with her when he was married. There was one thing in her life that Penny had never really been any good at. Lying. She'd wanted to tell him the truth at the time and here was her chance.

'I'm glad you brought that up. If you'd stayed around a bit longer and not jumped to conclusions, you would have met the man I was with that night. My father.'

'Ha! You expect me to believe that?'

'Why don't you ask Sarah, the sister who was on duty that night?'

'You might have just told her the man was your father. How would she know who he was?'

Penny was dumbfounded. 'You mean, you have no idea who my father is?'

Sam shook his head. 'Should I?'

Penny shrugged, recovering her composure. 'I guess not, considering you haven't been at this hospital for a good ten years or so but you did your internship under him. Sir Horace Hatfield, neurosurgeon. Ring any bells?'

Now it was Sam's turn to look dumbfounded. 'Sir Horace Hatfield is your father?'

Penny nodded, a smug smile on her face.

'I should have guessed.' Sam was on the attack again. 'Now I know where you get your stubbornness from.'

'Thank you. I'll pass on your regards.' Penny was now completely angry. 'Now, are you going to listen to what I have to say about Karen Deluth or not?' she yelled.

He walked back to his desk and sat down. 'There's no need to yell, Dr Hatfield.'

Great, Penny thought. We're back to the sarcasm. She whipped the X-rays from the packet and stalked over to his viewing machine.

'The external fixator that is currently on her leg is making absolutely no progress and I'm sure it has jammed. I remembered what you'd said about the new external fixator that was presented at the conference. The one that's guaranteed not to jam. Is it possible to get hold of that fixator and fast?'

'Sure.' His voice was back to its usual calmness— the professional was now in complete control. 'I'll ring a colleague in Melbourne and find out more details. Would you like to wait while I talk to him?'

'If you can get hold of him now. If not, I'd rather get some lunch.' She checked her watch. Almost half-past two. Great. That would mean that most of the food would be gone.

Sam flicked open his telephone directory and waited while the switchboard connected him. He got through to his colleague who was in an out-patient clinic. They talked for a few minutes before Sam replaced the receiver.

'He's going to send all instrumentation down with

an overnight courier and will fax through the operating manual so we can study it this evening.' Sam looked at her before adding, 'I'll have my secretary make a copy for you.'

Penny had just finished eating her dinner when the phone rang. She reached out a hand for the receiver.

'Hi, Penny.' Janey's cheerful voice assaulted her ears. 'How's everything going?'

'Fine. Just doing some late night study on a new technique. More to the point, how's the beautiful little boy?'

'Doing well. He should be able to come home in another few weeks but he's growing stronger every day.'

'Wonderful. How are Craig and the girls?'

'They're fine. Listen, the reason I've called is that Craig and I were wondering if you would be David's godmother?'

Penny could feel tears glistening in her eyes. 'Oh, Janey. I'd love to. Thank you so much for asking me.'

'Thank you for accepting. Craig's already asked Sam to be the godfather. It just seemed so appropriate, considering the role you two played in his appearance into this world.'

Penny's throat went dry at the mention of Sam's name. She swallowed convulsively and ended up asking Janey to wait while she got a drink of water.

'So, how are you and Sam going?' Janey asked when Penny returned to the phone.

'Uh. . .we're not,' she stammered then added quickly, 'Please don't ask me any questions, Janey. I don't want to talk about it.' Penny knew that she couldn't talk to her friend about Sam. After all, Janey was recovering from a premature birth, not to mention the long hours she would be spending at the hospital with baby David.

'That's too bad. Sure, I won't press. Anyway, I'd better let you get back to your reading. Take care.'

Penny sat in silence for at least ten minutes after Janey had hung up. She willed herself not to cry and instead began concentrating on the fixator manual.

The fixator arrived the next morning as promised and Sam and Penny went over it with a fine-tooth comb.

'Everything seems to be in order.' Sam replaced the instrument in the sterilising tray. 'Would you mind taking this to Theatre with a copy of the operating manual as it stipulates the autoclaving times? Then explain to Karen the procedure we'll be performing this afternoon.'

Penny collected the instruments and manual and was at the door when he spoke quietly. 'Have you accepted the role of godmother to David?'

Penny didn't turn around at his question and kept her back to him she said a quick, 'Yes,' before leaving his office.

She deposited the items with the theatre staff and made her way to the ward.

'Hi, Karen. How are you feeling?' Penny drew the curtain around the bed.

'Hungry.' The woman smiled and Penny was thankful that her spirits were high.

'Professor Chadwick and I will be taking you to Theatre in a few hours. I'd like to explain the procedure to you but feel free to ask any questions.' Penny waited for Karen's nod, then continued.

'What we'll be doing is removing this external fixator—' Penny pointed to the jammed instrument '—and we'll be replacing it with a new fixator that is guaranteed not to jam. We will also be performing another small operation on your leg at the same time to allow bone lengthening to occur simultaneously.

'When you break your leg and have open cuts, or what we call soft tissue injuries, it's impossible to fix the break with a plaster cast because then the cuts become infected. Therefore we need a way to hold your leg in place so that the bone can knit together with callus formation.'

Penny pulled a piece of paper out of her pocket and drew a diagram of a leg with a break in it.

'With external fixation it takes about sixteen weeks for the bone to knit back together. No fancy stitching, just plain and purl,' Penny joked, raising a smile from Karen.

'Once the bone has united your leg will be about three centimetres shorter. We would then need to perform an operation whereby we make a cut further up in the healthy part of the bone, stretch your leg out those three centimetres and again fix this with an external fixator.'

Penny drew another picture of a leg with a cut showing the lengthened segment and the new bone that would fill the gap.

'How does it fill in the gap?' Karen asked, her eyes wide.

'With bone callus. Callus is a mass of blood and granulation tissue that contains bone-forming cells.' Penny retrieved an X-ray she had brought in with her and held it up to the light. 'If you look on this X-ray you can see a slightly opaque area. That's bone callus forming in the fracture.'

'Is that my leg?' Karen asked.

'No. This is an X-ray that we keep for teaching purposes. This second operation is called leg lengthening. You would then need to have the external fixator on for another sixteen weeks. Do you follow so far?'

Karen nodded and Penny continued.

'The operation Professor Chadwick and I will be performing this afternoon is not only to replace your existing fixator with a better one that doesn't jam—we will also be performing the leg lengthening operation.'

'Then I'd need to have two pieces of metal sticking out of my leg.'

'Not with this new fixator. It has a special attachment that not only allows us to fix your fracture but by inserting a few extra pins we can make a cut further up in the bone and begin leg lengthening at the same time that your fracture below is healing. Basically it means that the whole process will take sixteen to eighteen weeks instead of thirty-two to thirty-six weeks.'

'I'm sorry, Dr Hatfield, but could you tell me again what's wrong with this fixator I have on now?'

'Don't be sorry. I want to make sure you understand. It's jamming. That means that its not allowing the fracture to unite correctly. That's why we have to take it off.' Penny's pager began to beep and she hurriedly turned it off.

'If this new fixator is so good why couldn't I have had it put on in the first place?' Karen asked.

'Because this new fixator has only just been released onto the market. It is still in the process of being mass produced but Professor Chadwick has been able to pull a few strings and obtain one especially for you.

'I'd better answer my pager. Would you like me to come back in half an hour and go over it again? That way it will give you time to think up some more questions.'

'Thanks, Dr Hatfield. That'd be great.'

Penny left to answer her pager. Once she had dealt with the query she decided that if she didn't take a lunch break now she'd never get one.

CHAPTER EIGHT

KAREN DELUTH'S operation took Penny and Sam a bit longer than they'd anticipated. Delays always happened when you were working with new instruments. Penny had discovered that Sam had been on the telephone to his colleague in Melbourne for a few hours that morning, going over the finer points of the new external fixator.

Penny had been pleasantly surprised at Sam's disposition in the theatre. He was very courteous to all staff, including herself. She could tell that the rest of the staff were still wary but so long as the operation proceeded smoothly she didn't care how anyone behaved.

'I'm glad that's over,' said one of the theatre nurses as she walked into the female changing-rooms and opened her locker. 'I wasn't sure whether Steaming Sammy was going to blow his top or not.'

'I haven't heard that one before.' Penny couldn't resist chuckling at the nickname the theatre staff had given Sam. She continued changing, dying to get home and relax.

'Well, to tell you the truth, Penny. . .' the other woman came and sat down on the bench next to Penny's locker '. . .we all thought you and our dear professor were as thick as thieves. The tension is almost visible when the two of you are in the room. At first we weren't sure whether it was good tension or bad tension. Then one of the orderlies overheard your conversation outside the changing-rooms and the hospital grapevine has been buzzing ever since.'

'That's just what I need,' Penny groaned and sat down with a bump on the bench.

'So, come on, Penny. What's the story?' The other woman's eyes were sparkling with amusement. 'Or am I to guess, by your long face, that if there was anything between you, it's over? Already?'

Penny sighed. Now that the grapevine was buzzing there was no stopping it but she might as well give it a try.

'It's definitely over.' Penny stood and slipped her shoes on. Closing her locker, she laughed humourlessly. 'Maybe I should restart the gossip that Derek and I having an affair. At least that rumour is less painful.'

'Don't bother. No one ever believed that you and Derek were more than just friends.'

'That's what you think,' Penny sighed. 'Well, I'd better be on my merry way. See you later.'

Penny arrived home to find her answering machine bursting with messages. There was one from her father, two from Janey and one from Derek. She decided to call Janey first, hoping that her friend wouldn't mention Sam's name but secretly hoping she would.

'Hi, Craig,' Penny said into the receiver a few minutes later. 'How's everything?'

'Fine. David's put on more weight and the girls adore him. My wife's figure is beginning to return to normal and I've just been offered a partnership. What more could a man want?'

Penny chuckled. 'Congratulations—for everything. Is Janey free to talk?'

'She's just finished tucking the girls in and is on her way to the phone in the bedroom. Bye.' Craig hung up his extension as Janey came on the line.

'Hello. Long time, no speak to,' Janey joked.

'Yeah. A whole twenty-four hours. Why the frantic messages on my machine? Couldn't you wait to hear my sexy voice?' Penny laughed at her own joke and heard Janey sigh.

'There's someone else who'd like to hear your sexy voice.' Janey always got straight to the point whether she offended Penny or not. So, this call was about Sam. She wondered if Craig had been ordered to ring Sam and find out more details.

'Who is it this time? You haven't been taping our conversations and playing them back to Craig's single workmates again?' Penny tried to make light of the situation, hoping to play for a little extra time against Janey's attack.

'You know exactly who I'm talking about, Penelope Hatfield.'

'Ooh, my full name. You must be mad,' Penny teased.

'What's going on? Why have you called it off with Sam? Did he do something wrong?'

'Now, let me think. Heartache, I needed to, and no. Does that satisfy your curiosity?'

'No it does not!' Janey yelled down the receiver. 'If I was in the same city as you, Penny, I'd come over and knock some sense into you.'

Penny sighed, trying to keep calm. It wasn't easy when your best friend was yelling at you. Nor when you were still madly in love with the man you didn't want to see because he was married.

'Look, Janey, I've already told you that I don't want to discuss it.'

'You sound upset.' Janey's voice took on a tone of calm urgency. 'Why are you upset?'

'I don't know.' Penny reached into her pocket for a

handkerchief. 'I just am. Everything is so confusing right now.'

'Can't you tell me about it?' Janey urged.

'Not yet. I still need more time.'

'More time for what? To get over him? Do you love him, Penny?'

Penny smiled through the tears that were silently streaming down her face. 'Why do you always have to ask three or four questions at once? It makes them very difficult to answer.'

'Just answer the last one, then. Do you love Sam?'

Penny tried to tell her friend the truth. Tried to say aloud that, yes, she loved Sam with all of her heart, but an enormous lump had blocked her throat. The only sound she was able to emit was a loud sob.

'Oh, Penny,' Janey soothed but it wasn't any good when she was at least seven hundred kilometres away.

'I have to go, Janey. I'll talk to you later.'

'No. Wait. . .'

Penny couldn't wait. She replaced the receiver and once the line was free she took the phone off the hook to prevent Janey from calling back. Again the tears began to flow, Penny's shoulders shaking as the heart-wrenching sobs racked her body. Why did he have to be married? Why?

Slowly she calmed herself down, taking deep breaths and blowing her nose. Things would have to change, she told herself sternly. Work was her only escape. Working hard would see her through this heartbreak. If she concentrated all of her energies on work then maybe, just maybe, she'd come out of this ordeal in one piece.

That was exactly what she did. Penny was all business. She stayed at the hospital until she was too tired to do anything but go home and sleep. Her paperwork was brought up to date and completed, much to the satisfaction of the ward clerical staff.

She began studying for her Fellowship exams, which she would have to take in another eleven months. Her long hours spent in the hospital library annoyed Derek, who was due to sit the exam with her.

'You make me feel guilty for partying instead of studying,' he complained one evening, almost three weeks after she had taken her 'work until you drop' vow. They were in the registrar's office and Derek had just completed an operating list. Penny, as was becoming customary for her, was buried in a textbook.

'Don't feel guilty.' She stood and stretched her cramped muscles. 'I need something to occupy my thoughts and studying seems the best solution. I promise I'll tell you everything I learn.' She smiled as she made the 'cross your heart' motion.

'Penny.' Derek pulled her down into the chair opposite him. 'I'm beginning to worry about you. He's not worth the punishment you're putting yourself through. You've lost weight, you're not eating properly and you've got dark circles under your eyes so I'll conclude that you're not sleeping.'

'I know.' She ran a hand through her hair before standing to pace the room. 'It's the only solution to my problem. Work will see me through. It's bad enough that I still run into him almost every day. He ignores me and I ignore him—on a personal level, I mean. It would be impossible to ignore each other on a professional level. I can just see it now.' She gave a snort of ironical laughter. 'The two of us passing messages through patients. Excuse me, Mrs so and so—' Penny pretended she was standing beside a patient '—could you please tell Professor Chadwick that I agree with his diagnosis?'

'Now I know you're mad.' Derek smiled, the concern for his friend still evident in his face. 'You're talking to yourself and imaginary patients!'

Penny slumped down into the chair and buried her head in her hands. 'Oh, Derek, it hurts so much. I really do love him.'

Derek placed a hand on her shoulder. 'I know what you need.' He waited for her to look up before he continued. 'You need a night out on the town with yours truly.'

'No, I don't. I wouldn't be very good company.' She shook her head.

'Well, you obviously don't give me very much credit. I'm one of your best friends. I know if Janey were here she'd probably have taken you out shopping and you would now be broke with a wardrobe full of clothes that you would probably never wear.'

Penny smiled at the thought. Derek knew Janey almost as well as she did.

'Now if, on the other hand, you let me take you out you will definitely not end up broke with a wardrobe full of clothes. You will end up smiling and even, perhaps, laughing. You never know, you might even enjoy yourself.' He held up a hand as she opened her mouth. 'No need to tell me I'm right. Just tell me what time I should pick you up tomorrow night?'

Tomorrow was Friday and Penny had been looking forward to reading chapter eleven of the text which sat in front of her. Compared to Derek's offer, the reading now began to appear extremely boring. Why shouldn't she let Derek take her out? He was right—she needed it.

'Seven-thirty,' she announced at last, knowing that he had watched the emotions play across her face.

'That's my girl. It shall remain a mystery as to where we shall go but do not fear, Cinderella, you shall go to the ball and enjoy it as well.' He tapped her on the head with an imaginary 'fairy godmother' wand and Penny laughed.

'And you were worried about me?'

Penny finished at the hospital on time and went home to have a leisurely shower before deciding what to wear. Derek had told her not to dress up too much so the black dress she had bought with Janey was out of the question. She eventually decided on her black crêpe pants, white T-shirt and a short black vest. She slipped her feet into black sling-backs and waited for her date to arrive.

Derek was late as usual and arrived just before eight. He presented Penny with a beautiful bunch of red and yellow gerberas and she admired them with delight.

'Derek, they're lovely. I'll put them in water and then we can go.' It only took a moment to arrange the flowers in a vase and position it on her dining-room table.

'Aren't you going to smell them?'

'They don't have any scent, silly.'

He shrugged. 'I'm glad you like them. After all, this is ''spoil Penny night'' tonight.'

Penny laughed and followed him out of the door. She climbed into his gun-metal grey Ferrari and they zoomed off toward the city.

'So, can you tell me now where we shall be dining this evening?' Penny grinned, getting into the spirit of enjoyment.

'Thai. There's a new restaurant in Unley that has come highly recommended.'

'By who?'

'Cindy-Lou.' Derek shot her a quick glance and together they laughed.

'Have you broken it off with her yet?'

'Yes. I took your advice and ended it. She called me a few days ago to flaunt her new lover in my face. She said he'd taken her to a very exclusive Thai restaurant in Unley and that Henry was more of a man than I'd ever be. I let her think she was right.'

'How gallant of you. So Henry's the new lover?'

'Yes. You'd think that I'd never taken the woman anywhere the way she was carrying on.'

'Is that bitterness that I detect?' Penny teased.

'Definitely not. I just let her rant and rave and sounded forlorn when inside I was grinning like a Cheshire cat.' He slowed the car and turned into a parking area. 'But enough about my ex-girlfriends. Tonight you are the belle at my ball.' He quickly climbed out before coming around to open Penny's door. 'Shall we?'

Penny linked her arm with Derek's and together they entered the restaurant. Their discussion ranged over various topics from their current patients right back to medical school memories. Penny could feel herself unwinding, the tension of the past few weeks dissipating under Derek's charming company.

'Cindy-Lou was right,' Penny said between mouthfuls of her peanut chicken. 'The food is exquisite.'

'If there was one thing she was good at, it was choosing restaurants.' Derek smiled and Penny knew that this was yet another romance Derek had managed to come through unscathed.

'One day, my friend—' Penny set her fork down and looked at him '—some woman is going to come along and knock you off your feet. You'll be so confused that for the first time in your life you won't have a clue what to do about it.'

'She can definitely knock me off my feet,' Derek

joked, 'but I sincerely doubt the confusion part. No woman will ever affect me like that. I'm always in control.'

Penny smiled a knowing smile. 'It will happen, Chalmers, and when it does I'll be there in the back ground chanting, "I told you so".'

'Dream on, Hatfield. Just because you've fallen in love that doesn't mean it suits everyone and besides. . .'

Penny felt all of the colour drain out of her face. She risked one more glance over Derek's shoulder before she turned frightened eyes back to him.

'What's wrong? I've done it again, haven't I? I've put my foot in it. I'm sorry, Penny, I was only joking around when I said you'd fallen in love and that it wasn't for everyone. I didn't mean to bring up memories of Sam or even mention his name, which I've just done. Oh, heck, I'm only opening my mouth to change feet.'

'He's here.' Penny swallowed convulsively and reached for her wine glass, hoping that its liquid would sooth the stabbing pains she was feeling in her heart.

'Who's here?' Derek started to turn and Penny quickly reached out a hand to touch his arm.

'No. Don't turn around or he'll notice us,' Penny said nervously.

'Who?' Derek asked again.

'Who do you think? Sam.'

'Sam's here? In this restaurant?' Penny watched as realisation dawned on Derek's face.

'Yes.'

'Is he with anyone or by himself?'

'I'd like to leave now.' Penny took the serviette from her lap and placed it gently on the table. 'Maybe he won't see us but we have to leave *now*.'

'All right, all right, keep your shirt on.' He signalled

the waiter and asked for their account. 'Why don't you go out to the car and wait there?' Derek suggested.

'Good idea.' Penny rose and picked up her purse. She'd turned and had taken a few steps toward the door when the deep baritone voice broke through her resolve.

'Good evening, Derek. Fancy seeing you here.'

Penny stopped, her back still to the men, and for a moment she thought an escape might be possible. Maybe Sam hadn't seen her yet but her thoughts were cut short.

'Good evening, Penny.'

She turned then to look at him. He was dressed in dark green drill pants with a khaki designer shirt. Penny felt her knees weaken and her heart pound faster. Her gaze continued to travel the length of him before her eyes came to rest on his. She read desire and hunger in his eyes and knew that hers were a mirror image.

She forced herself to lower her gaze, breaking the electrifying contact that she was sure the entire restaurant could see. Realising that if she didn't do something to support her knees soon, she'd end up a crumpled heap in the middle of the floor, Penny took the steps necessary to walk back to her chair and lean her hands on the back of it.

Derek had now paid for their meal and was standing as well. Penny could read his uncertainty at what to do next. Sam decided that for all of them.

'Aren't you going to say hello?' He looked at Penny, blatantly ignoring Derek.

'Hello.' There, she'd said it. What more did he want?

'How was the food?'

'Wonderful.' Her answer was curt. All she wanted to do was to get out of there.

'It was nice to see you, Sam.' Derek suddenly came

to life. 'We've got another engagement to get to so you won't mind if we say goodnight.' He came around the table and put a hand under Penny's elbow to escort her.

'Say goodnight to the professor,' Derek whispered in her ear.

'Goodnight,' Penny said obediently before Derek ushered her out of the restaurant and into the car.

'What was the matter with you?' Derek asked quietly when they were on their way.

Penny covered her face with her hands. 'I don't know.'

'You had the perfect opportunity to show him that he means absolutely nothing to you. That you were over him. Out having a good time. No! Instead you behave like a tongue-tied teenager facing a rock 'n' roll star.'

Penny removed her hands and tried some deep breathing in the hope of keeping the tears at bay. Derek glanced across at her a few times before pulling up at a red light.

'You've really got it bad, haven't you? You are totally and hopelessly in love with him, aren't you?'

Penny could only nod.

'Well, then, why don't you go out and get him, Hatfield? Fight for him. Why didn't you just grab him and plant an earth-shattering kiss on his lips? That would have got his attention.'

'He was there with another woman,' Penny said softly. 'I think it was his wife.'

Derek gasped. 'Of all the nerve. To come over to our table to say hello to the woman he's been romancing while his wife is sedately seated at a table not more than ten feet away.'

'Thank you, Derek,' Penny said crossly. 'You're such a big help in affairs of the heart. You can go now—the light is green.' She indicated the traffic lights and Derek turned his attention back to the road.

'Want me to beat him up?' Derek offered after a moment's silence.

Penny laughed, her anger with Derek dissipating. 'Don't be ridiculous.'

'How do you know it was his wife? Have you seen her?'

'I've seen a picture of her when they were in medical school together. She had long blonde hair then. Tonight the woman he was with had short blonde hair.'

'You only saw the back of her?'

'Yes.'

'How do you know it was his wife, then? Many women have blonde hair.'

'If she wasn't his wife then he's even worse than I'd thought,' Penny finished sadly. 'Now, can we talk about something else?'

'Sure. We can try but regardless of what conversation we carry on you'll still be thinking about Sam so I thought we'd talk it out.'

'If that's your logic then we won't talk at all and I hope you're taking me home.'

'No. I'm taking you out dancing.'

'I don't want to dance. The last place I feel like being is on a crowded dance floor.' She paused before adding more sincerity to her voice. 'Please, Derek. Come back to my place for a coffee, if you must, but I don't want to go dancing.'

'OK.' He relented and kept quiet until they reached Penny's home.

Penny's answering machine was again bursting with calls. She hit the rewind button then the play button. Derek filled the kettle before unashamedly joining her to listen to the messages.

There was one from her mother, one from the duty intern and two from Janey. Penny called the hospital and spoke to the intern. After obtaining a progress report on Karen Deluth, she rang off. It was too late to call her mother and she wasn't at all certain that she wanted to speak with Janey.

'Why's Janey being so persistent about you calling her?' Derek asked as he helped himself to her kitchen and made the coffee.

'She thinks Sam and I make a good couple,' Penny told him and waited for the next round of questions to begin.

'Janey knows Sam?' Derek sat down on the chair with a bump and almost spilled his coffee. Penny filled him in on the details of her trip and how Craig and Sam were old friends. While she spoke she had no idea that her voice and expressions were conveying how gentle Sam had been when he'd played with the girls. Or how authoritative yet compassionate he'd been when Janey had been in labour.

'No wonder.' Derek drained his cup and set it down on the coffee-table.

'No wonder what?'

'No wonder you fell in love with him so fast. Look, Penny, I don't profess to know anything about love or what it does to a person. I do know that you are an extremely intelligent woman and that if you think about things for long enough you generally come to the right conclusion.'

'What are you saying?'

'From what you've told me this evening, Sam is a very decent man. You've had the rare opportunity to see him away from the hospital and discover a side to him that he obviously doesn't let too many people see. Give him a chance, Penny. Let him explain.'

Penny was silent for a while before she shook her head. 'He's married, Derek. How can he explain that? It's so straightforward.'

'Not all the time. Anyway, I'd better go.' He gathered the cups and took them to the kitchen. 'I've left you with the washing-up again,' he smiled before hugging her close. 'Think about it, Penny.'

'What? How you always manage to leave me with the dishes?' Penny joked, trying to lighten her mood.

'You know what I mean. Oh, I almost forgot to tell you.' Derek hit his forehead with the palm of his hand.

'Can I do that?' Penny reached up a hand but Derek fended it off.

'The Easter dance.'

'What about it?' Penny asked. She had read the posters that had been stuck up around the hospital. It was their annual Easter dance and was usually the gala affair of the hospital social calendar. Due to her depression she had firmly decided not to attend.

'I've managed to swap my take with Dr Markum.'

'You should have asked me. I'd be happy to do your take so you can go along and fraternise with all of the lovely young nurses.'

'No, no, my dear. I have better plans for you. Dr Markum needs to do the take so I can escort you. I've bought two tickets and I won't take no for an answer.'

'No.' Penny said emphatically. Derek laughed.

'I said I won't take no for an answer. No doubt you've got something flashy tucked away in your wardrobe that you could wear. You've got two weeks to pull yourself together and then on Easter Saturday we'll launch you back into society.'

'You make me sound like a ship!'

'Let's see if the ship has anything to wear.' He turned and headed toward her bedroom. She followed him but couldn't match his long strides. By the time she arrived at her room he had her wardrobe doors flung open and was rifling through her clothes.

'Do you mind?' She stormed over and tried to shut the doors. Derek effortlessly pushed her out of the way.

'Well, well. What have we here?' He reached in and pulled out the black dress she'd bought with Janey. 'Still has the tag on it. There's only one person who could have talked you into buying such a sexy dress. I'll have to ring Janey and congratulate her,' Derek teased.

He held the dress up against a furious Penny. 'It will look perfect. Although your expression has got to change. If you walk into the ball looking at people like that you'll scare them away.'

'Derek Chalmers, hang that dress back up and get out of my room,' Penny fumed. Derek chuckled but did as she asked. She followed him back through the living-room and into the kitchen.

'I thought you were leaving?' she asked as he filled the kettle and plugged it in again.

'That's right. Kick me out just because I tease you.'

'I will. Now please go home.' She almost pushed him to the door.

'Do you have the right shoes, bag and jewellery to go with that dress?'

'Goodbye, Derek. I'll see you tomorrow.' Penny gave him a gentle shove through the doorway and began to close the door. He stuck his foot in and poked his head around.

'Think about what I said?'

Penny finally managed to get the door shut. Men, she thought. It wasn't just Sam or Derek. It was all men. They were all infuriating!

CHAPTER NINE

'WELL, you'll be pleased to know,' Penny told the ward sister, 'that Professor Chadwick has agreed that it is time Mr Smithers moved on.'

'Fantastic!' The ward sister smiled happily. 'Just wait until I tell my staff. When does he go?'

'He'll be transferred to the rehabilitation hospital tomorrow morning.' Penny grinned back at her colleague.

'I wish Mr Smithers a speedy recovery,' the ward sister said, 'but I've just had so much trouble with him. I understand how serious Munchausen's syndrome is but, believe me, he's a downright pain in the butt to nurse.'

Penny patted the other woman's shoulder. 'He'll be out of your hair this time tomorrow.'

'Thanks for having a word with the Prof.'

'It was no trouble,' Penny sighed. 'Now, Maureen Brooker is due for discharge this morning. How has she been?'

'Fine. Carol has been working with her almost constantly and a restraining order has been taken out against her husband. If he so much as touches her again he'll be locked up in gaol.'

'I don't imagine he'd be too happy about that.'

'You're right,' Carol said as she came to stand beside Penny. 'Have you got a moment? There are some finer points of Maureen's discharge that I need to discuss with you.'

'Sure. Lead the way.' Penny followed Carol into her

cardboard-box office where they spent the next hour discussing the Brooker case.

'Would you mind bringing Professor Chadwick up to date on these latest events?' Carol asked as Penny stood to go.

Penny faltered, her hand on the doorknob. Yes, she would mind. The less amount of time she had to spend with Sam the better. Although it was her job to inform him of happenings such as these, Penny knew that she couldn't face him one on one, especially after last night. She still wasn't ready.

She turned to face Carol. 'Could you do it instead?'

Carol scrutinised her for a moment before nodding her head. Penny wasn't at all sure what Carol had seen and was more than relieved that the other woman would tell Sam.

'Thanks,' was all Penny said as she opened the door and left.

Feeling the need for a bit of cheering up, Penny dropped in to Mr Wilson's room.

'Hello, Dr Hatfield. How are you this fine morning?'

'It's good to see you so cheery.' Penny walked to the end of the bed and reached for his chart.

'You didn't answer his question, Dr Hatfield.' Mrs Wilson smiled at Penny. 'How are you?'

'Just great, Mrs Wilson,' Penny lied and could tell her audience didn't believe her. She gestured to Mrs Wilson's knitting. 'Who's this one for?'

'My youngest grandson. He's almost two and out-grows his clothes faster than I can knit them. He'll need something warm to wear this winter so I decided that now was the time to start.'

'What she means is—' Mr Wilson looked lovingly at his wife '—considering she has to come and babysit me every day she might as well catch up on her knitting. Stops her from getting bored.'

'Now, Barry. You know that's just not true.' Mrs Wilson reached out and patted her husband's hand.

Penny watched their interchange and smiled wistfully. 'You two behave exactly like my parents.'

'Wipe that misty look from your face, girl,' Mrs Wilson chided softly. 'You and your professor will make it through. Barry and I have been through some awful times together and it's those hard times that make our love that much stronger.'

Penny knew that she was blushing and cleared her throat. She looked earnestly down at Mr Wilson's chart which she still held in her hands. 'You were X-rayed yesterday?' She tried to sound all business and knew that she wasn't fooling anyone. Nevertheless, the Wilsons played her little game and, for that, she was grateful.

'That's right. The professor said that I'm not progressing as well as he originally thought.'

Penny glanced up at Mr Wilson to see his reaction. 'This news doesn't bother you?' she asked gently.

'Not at all. Our farm is being well looked after. Margaret is catching up with our daughter, not to mention making the most of the opportunity to spoil our grandchildren, and if it takes my old bones a bit longer than usual to heal then why worry? They're not going to heal any faster. Right?'

Penny couldn't help smiling. 'You're a model patient, Mr Wilson. I wish they were all like you.' She scribbled a note on his chart before replacing it at the foot of the bed.

'What are you up to this evening?' Mrs Wilson asked, not taking her eyes from her knitting. Penny stiffened but Mr Wilson's chuckle eased her.

'Margaret. You need to learn not to be so direct with people.' He turned his head to Penny. 'What my wife would like to know is would you be free to come and visit me this evening?'

'I'm going out on the town,' Mrs Wilson said earnestly. 'Debbie's taking me to the movies. Just the two of us.' The excitement was evident in her face.

'So, you see, I'll be all alone.' Mr Wilson smiled. 'Do you like playing cards?'

'I'd be delighted to come and visit you tonight. What time should I drop by?'

Penny dressed casually and arrived at the hospital at seven-thirty. She walked through the main entrance that led to the ward and, on rounding a corner, came face to face with Sam. They both stopped and looked at each other.

'You're working late, Sam,' Penny spluttered, not knowing what to say.

'I had some paperwork to catch up on. I was just going out for a bite to eat before continuing.' He hesitated. 'Would you care to join me?'

Penny lowered her head. If she looked at him for too long all reason would be thrown to the wind.

'Sorry. I have another appointment.'

'Another date with Derek?' His tone had changed to one of ice and Penny's eyes quickly made contact with his.

'No. I don't have another date with Derek, not that it would be any business of yours if I did.' Why did she let him rile her? 'For your information I have a lovely evening planned with. . .'

'I don't want to hear it,' he snapped.

'With Mr Wilson,' she continued, pleased that he looked contrite at her disclosure. 'His wife is having a night off and he's asked me to keep him company.'

'Pen.' Sam rested his hand on her shoulder. 'I'm sorry.' His eyes swept her figure, resting briefly on her breasts before he looked into her eyes. Penny shivered and Sam immediately dropped his hand.

'I'd better let you go.' His voice held a note of finality and Penny wondered if his words had a double meaning. She nodded before walking past him and quickly continued her journey to the ward.

'Dr Hatfield,' one of the ward nurses smiled as she entered the ward. 'What are you doing here?'

'I'm not here as a doctor, I'm here as a visitor. I'll be playing cards with Mr Wilson for the next few hours if anyone is looking for me.' Penny went into his room and closed the door.

'Right on time and you look lovely, Dr Hatfield.' Mr Wilson smiled.

'If I'm about to beat you at cards you'd better call me Penny.'

'Likewise, you should call me Barry because I'll be the one wearing the victory smile.'

'You are ruthless when your wife's not around to keep you in check,' Penny joked and set up the bed-table to make sure Barry was comfortable. They played a round of gin rummy and were on their fourth hand when Penny asked, 'Who's looking after your farm?'

'My youngest son.'

'How many children do you have?'

'Five. The oldest is thirty-eight and the youngest is twenty-six. Paul is his name and he's just finished studying agriculture. He calls me every day with updates and keeps telling me this is his chance to take over and arrange to put me and Margaret into a retirement home.' Barry chuckled and Penny knew that he shared a great sense of humour with his children.

'I only have one brother and for him I'm ever grateful. I was an only child for thirteen years and although it was nice to have my parents' attention it was often very lonely.'

'Sam told me that your father was a famous doctor.'

Penny looked up from her cards at the mention of Sam's name. She swallowed before replying. 'That's right. He was a neurosurgeon before his eyes gave up on him. A truly brilliant man, my father.'

'You have a lot of respect for him.' It was a statement, not a question.

'Yes, and for my mother as well. She was a nurse who gladly gave up her career to care for her daughter and husband. They're remarkable people.'

Barry put his cards down and took Penny's from her hands. 'They've obviously raised you well. You're a smart woman, Penny, and what I'm about to say to you may sound as though I'm meddling but Margaret and I can't go on seeing you punish yourself the way you have been the past few weeks.'

Penny remained silent, unsure whether she was going to like what she was about to hear.

'Sam comes in to see us almost daily. Strangely enough, the two of you never pop in at the same time. Margaret and I have seen it all before. Paul is our only child who's not married so we've had a bit of practice at reading the signs.'

Penny opened her mouth to protest.

'No, love. Hear me out. When Sam returned from his little holiday he was relaxed and happy. He didn't tell us any explicit details of his time away but just at the mere mention of your name a spark would light in his eyes and a warmth radiated his face. You have exactly the same reaction when you say his name. You love him, don't you?'

Penny could only nod. Was she that obvious? If Sam hadn't said anything and neither had she, how did the Wilsons know what was going on?

'The eyes are the window to the soul,' Barry said softly as though reading her mind. 'Especially if you know what to look for.' He reached out and took her hand. 'What's wrong? What happened? The spark has gone out of both of you and it saddens us to see true love being thrown away.'

Penny didn't know what to say and could feel tears beginning to prick at her eyes. She lowered her head as though to shield the pain.

'Have you confronted him with the problem you've found? Given him a chance to explain? Were you moving too fast? The only way you get through relationships is to communicate. Talk to him. Things aren't as black and white as they seem.'

Penny pulled out a handkerchief and blew her nose. Barry's words were almost identical to Derek's. Maybe someone was trying to tell her something.

'I'm sorry, lass. I didn't mean to upset you. The lecture's over but think about it. Now, how about we play a little canasta to take your mind off things?'

The rest of the evening progressed without a hitch and Penny left just after ten o'clock, feeling happier than she had in days.

Just as she pulled into her driveway her car gave a shudder before returning to its usual idle. She switched it off and made a mental note to book it in for a service. Her answering machine was blinking furiously and again there was a message from Janey.

'Penny.' Janey's voice was matter-of-fact. 'I'm going to keep calling you until you ring me back and tell me what is going on. I don't want to meddle but you're forcing me to. I'm only doing it because I love you. Please call.'

Penny filled the kettle and plugged it in. She was so confused. Everything Barry Wilson had said tonight made sense and everything Derek had said last night made sense. Even Janey, who was in another state, was begging her to talk about it.

She made herself a cup of tea and carried it into her room. She just needed more time. More time to think.

The next week flew by and between work, visiting her parents and studying when she wasn't doing anything else Penny was exhausted. She had also done a lot of soul-searching and, considering that the advice she had been forced to listen to was generally the same, she conceded that maybe Sam was worth fighting for.

Penny had only thought of herself. How *she* was going to cope without Sam. He was a married man— she had proof of that—but where was his wife? That photograph had been taken almost fourteen years ago. Anything could have happened. Maybe they were separated or even divorced. She might not live in the same country. The possibilities were endless.

Sam had taken her to his home, the home where he had grown up. Penny didn't remember seeing any female paraphernalia and the only photographs had been of Sam and his parents.

Her spirits began to lift but then she remembered the blonde lady at the restaurant with Sam. There was living proof that his wife existed. He'd taken her to a restaurant. Even divorced people can remain friends, a little voice inside her heart spoke out.

She ran a hand through her half-dry hair. It looked as though her only option of discovering the truth was to confront Sam and let him explain. She looked at herself in the mirror and smiled a watery smile.

'Nothing ventured, nothing gained,' she told her reflection and continued to put her make-up on.

She finished dressing and went out to her car. Buckling up, she inserted the key into the ignition and turned it. The car's engine turned over then died. Nothing! She unbuckled the belt and popped the bonnet. She knew absolutely nothing about cars and having a look around when she'd lifted the bonnet didn't make her feel any better. She'd completely forgotten to book it in for a service and now she was going to pay the price.

Penny closed the bonnet before relocking the car and going back inside. She phoned for a taxi then had Derek paged to let him know she was going to be late for the ward round.

It was half an hour later before she slipped into the ward round, hopefully unnoticed. Derek shifted so that he was standing beside her.

'What took you so long?' he whispered out of the corner of his mouth. 'I tried to cover for you but the Prof's out for blood.'

Penny groaned at his words and rolled her eyes heavenward.

'Dr Hatfield.' Sam's voice broke through the crowd and everyone turned to look at her. 'Nice of you to join us.'

'I'm sorry, Professor. I had car trouble,' she stammered. He waved her excuses away and continued with the round. Penny turned to Derek and comically wiped her forehead. 'Whew! That was close.'

Derek smiled. 'Come on,' he whispered before clutching her arm and escorting her to the next patient.

They were in the registrar's office an hour later discussing her dead car.

'I've absolutely no idea what's wrong with it. It

made a whirring sound then died.'

'Sounds like the spark plugs are dirty,' Derek said and sipped his coffee. 'So, how has the "I'm going to work myself into the ground" routine been going?'

'I'm exhausted but I'm almost happy.' Penny put her elbow on the desk and leaned her head in her hand.

'Only "almost"?'

'I've figured out what to do about Sam. You were right, Derek. I'll confront him and ask him straight out.'

'Ask him what?' Derek teased.

'Whether he's married or not. What else am I supposed to ask?'

'Considering your usual direct way of questioning, wouldn't it be better to build up slowly?'

'What are you talking about?'

'For the past few weeks you've played it cool. You've ignored him and treated him like dirt.'

'He's treated me the same way,' Penny protested.

'I know, I know. What if he has now decided that he *doesn't* want anything to do with you?'

'But Barry Wilson said. . .'

'Mr Wilson? You've discussed this with a patient?' Derek asked incredulously.

'No. Well, not really. He discussed hypothetical situations with me. He says he can tell, just by looking at the two of us, that we're madly in love and that if I truly love Sam he'd be worth fighting for. Regardless of the problems.'

'Good luck to you.' Derek went to the sink. 'It's your turn to do the washing-up, Penny.' He was laughing at his own joke when there was a knock at the door. Sister poked her head around.

'Oh, good. You're both here. The professor would like to see the two of you in his office immediately.'

'Do you know what it's about?' Derek asked as he reached for his white coat.

'No. Sorry.'

A few minutes later Derek rapped on Sam's office door and a brisk, 'Enter,' was heard. Sam wasn't the only person in his office and he gestured for Penny and Derek to be seated at the conference table.

'Now that everyone's here, I'll begin. There has been an emergency call from Roxby Downs. A miner has been injured and is still trapped inside the mine. They have a first-aid officer on site who has been down to do a preliminary check. He's fairly sure that the right arm and leg are broken but also said that a large boulder was lifted off the man's hip and pelvic region.

'The doctor in Roxby Downs is apparently at an outback station on an emergency call and won't be able to get there until some time this afternoon.

'Because the extent of his injuries is mostly ortho-paedic, the Royal Flying Doctor Service would rather that we attend the patient direct. They're organising for their aircraft to be ready and waiting at the airport as soon as we get more information.'

'Do you know exactly how it happened?' Penny asked.

'All I've been told is there was some sort of rock fall after a routine blasting procedure had been carried out. Our patient was beneath the rock fall.'

'Is there a record of any allergies?' Dr Phil Werner, the anaesthetist, asked.

'We haven't received that information yet.'

'What about blood type?' Phil was furiously taking notes.

'That information should be here soon. They're fax-ing through his company medical profile.'

'What's the next step, Professor?' Theatre Sister Rosemary Williams asked.

'We wait for further updates but I want everyone to be on standby. Chalmers—' he turned to Derek '—you'll stay here. I want the theatre set up and ready to go the minute we arrive at the hospital. Hatfield, you'll be coming with me. Gather up all necessary equipment.

'The moment we get the word to move we'll be taken by ambulance to the airport and on a plane for Roxby Downs. It could be another half-hour before we need to go so I suggest you all get something to eat, make any necessary phone calls to your families, get changed into the hospital retrieval team flying suits and have the medical equipment ready to go.'

'How long do you anticipate we'll be away?' Rosemary asked.

'I've no idea at this stage. I'd say for the rest of the day and by the time we finish in Theatre, who knows what the time will be? That's it, I'll see you all back here in half an hour.'

CHAPTER TEN

OVER an hour later the Royal Flying Doctor Service's King Air B200C was on its way to Roxby Downs.

Penny was sitting next to Sam who had his head tilted back on the headrest with his eyes shut. Rosemary and Phil were seated in front of them, their voices low as they talked.

She took the opportunity to study Sam, her heart filling with love as her eyes roved over his face. His expression wasn't one of relaxation and she understood that he was concentrating on the upcoming tasks he would have to perform.

She longed to hold him to her, to kiss away the small furrow that creased his brow and to tell him that she loved him and that nothing would ever separate them again. Penny turned to look out the window, suppressing her thoughts about Sam, and focussed on the poor man who was trapped down the mine.

'Penny.' Sam spoke her name quietly, his breath fanning her neck. She turned to him and looked into his eyes. She saw pain, confusion and a strong spark of desire. Her mind was temporarily drawn back to what Barry Wilson had said. 'The eyes are the window to the soul.'

She felt compassion and excitement dwell within her as she longed to tell him the truth. Nervously she cleared her throat.

'Sam, now is not the time or the place but we. . .'

'I know,' he interrupted her. 'We need to talk.'

Penny watched in a daze as his hand reached out to squeeze hers gently.

'We'll work it out. But for now we should concentrate on Mr Anderson.' He glanced at his watch. 'We should be able to see the township of Roxby Downs any moment now.'

Penny looked out the window and was amazed at the amount of red dirt. It was everywhere. As the small plane continued its journey buildings seemed to appear from nowhere and soon the entire township was set out before them. The hot sun glinted off the tinned roofs of many houses, making the township sparkle like a rare jewel in the surrounding Australian desert. Amazingly enough, she could even see a bright blue swimming pool, accompanied by the greenness of grass.

To their left was the mining centre. At least seven long metal storage sheds sat firmly in place, well-worn car tracks defined the dirt into roads and she could see a tunnel that obviously led underground to the mine. As they lost altitude the red barrenness seemed to engulf her, capturing Penny effortlessly under its spell. Roxby Downs really was an oasis in the desert.

The wheels touched down on the graded dirt of the airstrip. Sam's hold on her hand continued. From it she drew the strength she would need to get through these next few hours.

An ambulance met them and, with the siren wailing, the vehicle drove them to the mine site.

'Right,' Sam addressed his staff. 'Let's go over things once more. The patient's name is James Anderson. He's thirty-seven and married with three children. As far as we know—' Sam looked directly at Phil '—he's not allergic to anything, which should make your job a bit easier. The rock fall has been cleared away and the first-aid officer is still in attendance. Rosemary, Penny and I will need you at the ready.'

They clambered out of the ambulance and were met by Mr Krellon, the mine superintendent. The doctor from Roxby Downs was still uncontactable on a remote homestead outside Andamooka, delivering a baby.

Mr Krellon gave out the necessary attire for entering the mining area—large blue overalls that were covered in red dirt, enormous black gumboots, hard hats with a light on top and a heavy belt that carried the battery pack for the hat light.

Penny and Rosemary had the hardest time of all, considering the overalls were definitely not made for women. The crotches came to somewhere between their knees and the ends of the trouser legs were rolled up a few times before being stuffed into the oversized gumboots. Penny glared daggers at the amused expression on Sam's face as his eyes roved over her bulky figure.

'Not a word,' she told him curtly and saw him swallow the laughter. 'Shouldn't we load the four-wheel drives with the equipment?'

He nodded and soon they were bundled into the vehicles that would take them four hundred metres below the surface to where James Anderson needed their assistance.

Getting into the four-wheel drives was an ordeal in itself. Because the overalls were so big Penny couldn't swing her leg up to the small step which would enable her to pull the rest of her body onto the seat. After a few attempts Sam grabbed her firmly around the waist and with no effort at all lifted her onto the seat before climbing in beside her. Rosemary and Phil went in the other four-wheel drive, the equipment being shared between the two vehicles.

Penny was amazed by the tunnel, or service decline portal, as their driver called it. It had huge, curved cement walls similar to a dam construction. They passed through the entranceway and were underground in a tunnel at least four and a half metres high and six metres wide.

'Can you give us a more detailed account of what exactly happened to James Anderson?' Sam asked their driver.

'As far as I know, after the blasting and while James was checking the samples for their ore content. . .'

'We were told he was a miner. Is he a geologist?' Penny interrupted.

'That's right. Maybe I should explain the procedure first. What happens here is first they drill a development face in the rock. Explosive charges are placed down these holes and the rock blasted away. A geologist then checks a few samples for the ore content before a load-haul dump truck scoops it all up into an orepass truck. This truck then delivers the ore to the loading station where it is crushed and fed through onto a large conveyor belt.

'What happened to James was a fault in the rock they were blasting. The weakness in the rock should have appeared in the tests but it obviously went undetected. After the blasting James was sampling the ore when a rock fall, just a small one, started.

'Everyone else managed to get clear but James's leg was pinned by a rock and then a few more fell on him. At first they thought he was dead before someone took his pulse.'

They all remained quiet for the remainder of the trip, caught up in their own thoughts. Major trauma retrieval was extremely stressful but the stress wasn't nearly as great when you knew that the people you were working with were highly trained professionals in their specialised field.

A million scenarios cluttered Penny's mind as to what they would find when they eventually reached Mr Anderson. What minor surgery would they need to perform in order to stabilise him for retrieval to the city hospital? The possibilities were endless.

They drove for at least another five minutes before Penny could see lights ahead. A few more metres and they would be ready to burst into action. The company's first-aid officer was still beside the injured man, taking his pulse.

They disembarked from the four-wheel drives, which was a lot easier than climbing into the vehicles. All Penny had to do was flip her legs over the edge of the seat and slide down. This would have worked fine if she hadn't landed in a puddle of water, spraying droplets over Sam's overalls.

He smiled at her before unloading their equipment onto the uneven, wet and muddy ground. Penny could feel herself beginning to sweat and turned to their driver. 'What's the temperature down here?'

'Usually about forty degrees Celsius and about ninety-eight per cent humidity due to being below the water table.' He shrugged. 'A person gets used to it.'

'What's the latest?' Sam asked as they all settled around the patient.

'He's just slipped back into unconsciousness. When he was conscious he was a little disorientated but seemed to recollect who he was and what had happened. He's been on oxygen since nine o'clock, which was shortly after the accident happened.'

'You've managed to stop all external bleeding?' Sam asked, all the while examining the supine patient.

'Yes.' The first-aid officer moved aside to let the

professionals take over. Penny noticed a look of relief
cross his face and she smiled at him.

'You've done a good job,' she praised, before setting
up the saline drip.

Rosemary reached for the scissors and cut away the
tough, wet material of the overalls from the uninjured
leg. Phil knelt and delved into his bag. He extracted a
vial of pethidine and drew it into the syringe. Rosemary
swabbed an area of James's thigh before Phil injected
the drug. Within seconds they saw their patient's face
relax as the drug took effect.

'Pulse? Blood pressure?' Sam asked quietly but
directly.

'Pulse is quite fast,' Rosemary responded efficiently.
She crouched down beside James's left arm and
reached for the sphygmomanometer. 'Blood pressure
ninety over sixty.'

Penny checked the open wounds and changed the
dressings. Sam was murmuring a list of injuries to her
as he continued his thorough examination. 'Dislocated
right shoulder, fractured right ulna and radius, fractured
right femur, fractured right tibia and fibula and fourth
and fifth metatarsals are broken.'

'I thought his shoulder might be dislocated. Are you
going to pop it back in?' the first-aid officer asked and
Penny shook her head.

'We can't relocate the shoulder until it's been
X-rayed. If the humerus or clavicle,' she explained
pointing to her upper arm and shoulder, 'are fractured
then we'll need to treat it differently.'

Penny helped Rosemary set up the stretcher before
they began work on the inflatable immobilising splints.
Twenty minutes later James was secured onto the
stretcher before Phil and Sam loaded him onto the
four-wheel drive.

The journey out didn't seem to take as long as their initial one. When the four-wheel drives had come to a complete stop outside, a young woman rushed over as James was carried across to the waiting ambulance.

'James, James.' Her voice was wrought with emotion, her face stained with tears. Penny reached out a hand to her and gently pulled her away from the stretcher.

'Mrs Anderson?' Penny waited for the affirmative response. 'I'm Dr Hatfield. We will need to transport your husband immediately to Adelaide where we can operate on him. You are more than welcome to accompany us on the flight but if you have children or things you need to attend to I can have a flight organised for you.'

'Everything's organised,' Mr Krellon inserted, handing Penny a small bag. 'I advised Mrs Anderson to pack a few hours ago and to arrange care for her children.'

'Great.' Penny smiled her appreciation to Mr Krellon before turning to Mrs Anderson. 'Well, if you'd like to come with me.' Penny ushered her over to the waiting ambulance. The retrieval team undressed from their mining attire before boarding the ambulance. There was a short drive back to the airstrip before James was lifted through the open double doors of the plane and strapped in securely. Rosemary sat beside him and tended to his wife.

'I asked Mr Krellon to contact the hospital and let them know we're leaving,' Sam said once they were all seated. 'Our pilot will radio ahead to the airport to check that the ambulance will be waiting. Rosemary, I need obs done every ten minutes.'

'Yes, Prof.'

The journey back seemed to take for ever but soon they were zooming their way toward the hospital in a haze of flashing red lights. Derek met them at the casualty entrance to confirm theatre arrangements. James Anderson was wheeled toward the resuscitation bay where a portable X-ray machine and radiology staff were waiting to do their jobs. Penny, Derek and Sam made their way to the emergency surgical suite, where they changed into theatre garb.

An hour later they were well into the operation. Having established that there was no fracture to the clavicle or humerus, Sam had relocated the shoulder into its socket. The fractured femur had been fixed with a metal rodding technique down the cavity of the bone, while the tibia and fibula, as well as the ulna and radius, had been stabilised with plaster of Paris.

Upon closer examination of the X-rays, they discovered that James had a transverse fracture through the socket of the hip joint. Derek had left Theatre and gone to the out-patient clinic. Without either Penny or Sam, the clinic would be heavily delayed.

Penny watched as Sam made the incision along the anterior two-thirds of the iliac crest, continuing down to the midline only two fingerbreadths above the symphysis pubis. The anterior abdominal muscles were also incised from the iliac origin and the fracture exposed. Few words were exchanged as the operation proceeded without complication.

Once the fracture had been stabilised on the anterior side, the posterior approach was next. Sam made another incision approximately sixteen centimetres along the proximal side of the femur toward the greater trochanter, angling slightly posteriorly to the iliac crest.

They fixed the fracture with one posterior interfragmentary screw and a small pelvic reconstruction plate.

'Damn,' Sam muttered and Penny looked up. 'The superior gluteal artery and nerve are trapped between bony fragments at the greater sciatic notch.' He tilted his head back slightly so that the sister could wipe the perspiration from his forehead.

'Penny—' Sam focussed his attention back on the patient '—could you protect it while I carefully extract the fragments?'

All personnel in Theatre held their breaths until Sam slowly exhaled and looked at Penny.

'Right, Dr Hatfield.' His eyes sparkled and she could tell that he was smiling beneath his mask. 'Let's X-ray, then close.'

It was half an hour later when Penny took her gloves off and removed her surgical cap and mask. After Rosemary had helped her remove her gown, Penny slumped down into a chair, tilted her head back against the wall and closed her eyes. She was drained.

'I know how you feel.' Sam's soothing tones cut through the pounding that was going on inside her head. 'What a day!' She felt the movements as he sat down in the chair next to her and after a few moments' silence she opened her eyes and looked at him.

He was staring at her with a weary expression. She managed to dredge up a smile.

'You look how I feel.'

'You'd better go home and get some sleep.' He reached out a hand and patted her knee.

'Oh, no,' she gasped, raising a hand to her head. 'My car. I'd forgotten it was at home. Great.' The hand that had been on her head slapped down onto her thigh. 'Now I'll have to wait for a taxi.'

Sam smiled at her. 'Is that a hint?'

'No, not at all. I was just making an observation out loud.'

He chuckled. 'Sure.' He sounded as though he didn't believe her. 'Never mind. I'll drop you at home.

Get changed and I'll meet you in my office.'

Penny stayed where she was, her eyes travelling from his down to where his hand still rested on her knee. She began to blush and Sam's chuckle deepened.

'You don't have to worry about anything. I'm far too tired to ravish you, although I wouldn't mind raiding your refrigerator.' He stood and pulled her to her feet. 'Go. I'll write up the notes and see you in my office.'

She was too tired to argue and did as he asked. Ten minutes later Penny was outside his office, waiting for him. She didn't bother to shower, having decided to have one at home so she'd be clean and fresh for bed.

'Sorry,' Sam said as he rushed up the corridor. He quickly opened his office and disappeared inside. A few moments later he reappeared with his briefcase and jacket. 'Let's go.'

He seated Penny in the Jaguar and, as he turned the powerful car onto the nearly deserted streets, the soothing sounds of Mozart filled the air. Her next conscious thought was when Sam gently shook her, urging her to wake up.

'Where are your keys?' he asked and she reached into her handbag to retrieve them. He took them from her and, with one hand under her elbow, ushered her to the door.

The first thing Penny usually did when she arrived home was to fill the kettle and switch it on. She did this now, functioning on automatic pilot. Sam walked straight to her refrigerator and opened it.

'It's nice to see a well-stocked fridge,' he said as he began to take out various items.

'You're in luck. I only went shopping yesterday. Usually it's bare,' Penny said in a monotone as she pulled out a chair.

'Why don't you go and have a shower while I cook us something to eat?' He came and stood beside her and placed a hand on her forehead. 'You're a bit hot but it could just be fatigue setting in.' He kissed the top of her head before turning her by the shoulders. 'Go,' he ordered for the second time that night.

The shower made her feel slightly more in control of her senses and, after she'd dressed in her mid-thigh-length nightshirt, her stomach grumbled as the aroma of Sam's cooking filled the air.

'That smells wonderful,' she said, entering the room. 'Who taught you to cook? Or has Antonio dropped around again?'

He laughed and Penny's heart lurched. It felt good to be with him again and not feel pain. She suddenly realised that by him being here and enjoying her company that maybe, just maybe, she had a chance with him.

'Your answering machine seems to be bursting with messages,' he pointed out as he began to dish the food onto plates.

'It can burst.' She ignored the flashing red light. 'It's too late to call anyone back,' she replied, glancing at the clock, and was surprised to find it was almost midnight.

'Sit. Eat,' he commanded as she sat down. A plate of stir-fried beef and vegetables, served on a bed of white rice, was placed before her.

'You didn't tell me you were a gourmet cook.' Penny couldn't get the food to her mouth fast enough. 'This is terrific!'

'Why, thank you.' He smiled at the compliment, his eyes drooping slightly.

Penny put her fork down and looked at him. 'You're exhausted,' she said softly and he nodded.

'Do you mind if I sleep here tonight? I really am too tired to drive home.'

'Sure,' she said without hesitation. She resumed eating the delicious meal, wondering where the best place was for him to sleep. The couch was probably too short for his long frame and the floor would be too hard. He couldn't sleep in her bed, or could he? She blushed at the thought and bent her head to hide her face.

Sam chuckled and she realised that he'd been carefully watching her. 'Your facial expressions reveal far too much of your thoughts. I promise I'll do nothing else but hold you. Trust me.' He reached out a hand and squeezed hers briefly. 'We are really both quite exhausted and there is no alternative other than for me to risk driving home. Would you ever be able to forgive yourself if I had an accident?'

'That's emotional blackmail,' she stated before forking in the last mouthful of food.

'Never,' he said with mock innocence. 'Do you mind if I have a quick shower?'

'First you barge in here, eat my food, emotionally blackmail me into letting you stay and now you want to utilise my hot water and electricity?'

'Got it in one,' he smiled and stood. 'You can do the dishes.' He walked off and she rushed after him. Being the good hostess that she was now forced to be, she dug out a clean towel and pointed the way to the bathroom.

'And don't come out wearing just your towel,' she called after his retreating back.

'Why not? I thought you were too tired to try anything.'

'Sam!' she said indignantly and he laughed.

'The dishes await you,' he said before closing the bathroom door.

'I'm beginning to get a real complex about doing the dishes,' she mumbled to herself as she entered the kitchen. 'Maybe I'll buy a dishwasher.'

CHAPTER ELEVEN

PENNY woke with a start and quickly looked at the clock. Half-past ten! She was positive that she'd switched her alarm on. Picking up her clock, she looked at it through bleary eyes. Definitely half-past ten. Why had her alarm not sounded?

She sighed heavily, realising that she'd better get up and ring the hospital. Sam would be furious that she was late, especially as this made it two mornings in a row. Sam. Last night came flooding back to her and she checked the bed beside her. He wasn't there but the pillow definitely had an indentation in it. She hadn't been dreaming.

She stumbled out into the kitchen to find Sam dressed and at the stove cooking breakfast.

'Good morning,' he said cheerfully. 'Would you like some coffee?'

'Yes. How can you stand there and cook when it's half-past ten? We're supposed to have already completed a ward round and. . .'

'Calm down. I've called the hospital and notified them we'd be in for the afternoon list.'

'Who did you speak to?' Penny asked curiously while she sipped her coffee.

'My secretary and Chalmers.'

'You spoke to Derek?' Penny sat abruptly down into the chair.

'Yes. He seemed quite pleased that we were. . .' he paused and raised his eyebrows for emphasis '. . .together.'

161

'Yeah, he would,' Penny growled into her cup. She could just hear the 'I told you so's that were coming her way. He'd think he was so smart—that he'd been the one who had brought them back together.

Nothing has been resolved, a small voice inside Penny made her realise. Even though Sam had stayed here last night, they hadn't talked. She sighed again and ran her fingers through her short curls.

'You're not a morning person, are you?' he stated matter-of-factly as he put an omelette in front of her.

'How did you guess?' she grumbled. They ate in silence and shared the morning paper. They were really quite domesticated. It reminded Penny of their holiday at Janey's and how they had taken care of the girls. It all seemed so long ago. She'd been through so much heartache since then.

'Penny.' He broke through her thoughts and she looked at him. 'Do you feel like having that talk?' The moment the words were out of his mouth a faint beeping noise came from his briefcase. 'Great,' he said ironically as he went to his case and retrieved his pager.

'I won't be a moment,' he said and reached for the phone.

Penny felt as though the emotional roller-coaster ride was becoming bumpier. She had so loved having his arms around her whilst she slept. It had been difficult to banish the thought of his wife from her mind and just enjoy the sound of his breathing as he'd held her close.

'A friend of yours has come back for a visit,' Sam said when he'd replaced the receiver. 'Mark Shields has a humeral neck fracture. Derek's seen him and wanted to check if we could fit him in on our elective list this afternoon. Apparently, there's been a cancellation.'

'But he won't have fasted.'

Sam chuckled. 'Mark's friend—Steve, I think Derek said his name was—' and Penny nodded. 'Well, Steve hasn't let him eat anything just in case he had to have more surgery. The accident happened last night and it's taken until now for Steve to persuade Mark to come back into hospital. Apparently he was worried about the ''sheila'' treating him again.' Sam gave way to the mirth that had been building and Penny punched him playfully.

'Well, this ''sheila'' had better get ready.' She left the table and took her plate to the sink. 'You can do the dishes this time.'

It was almost half-past twelve when Sam dropped Penny at the hospital, telling her that he'd have to go home and change his clothes.

'Have a pleasant evening?' Derek sneaked up behind her and whispered in her ear the moment she set foot inside the casualty department.

She wanted to turn around and tell him that nothing had happened; tell him that nothing had been resolved and to take a swipe at him for teasing her. Instead, Penny swivelled slowly on her heel and said, 'Yes. Thank you for asking. Which cubicle is Mr Shields in?'

'OK. I won't tease you. . .for now.' He grinned and pointed down the corridor. 'He's in number six.'

'Thank you,' Penny turned and began walking.

'The X-rays should be back any minute now.' Derek caught up with her. 'Hey, where's Sam?'

Penny stopped again and glared at him.

'I wasn't teasing.' He held his hands palms outward in self-defence. 'Honest. I was just asking where our esteemed leader might be. Do you know where the Prof is, Dr Hatfield?'

Penny swallowed, knowing that her answer was going to set Derek off again.

'He's gone home to change then he'll be back.' She began walking.

'What's he going to change into? A werewolf? A vampire?'

Penny continued to ignore him and pushed the curtain aside to cubicle six. Mark Shields was on the bed and his mate, Steve, was sitting on the chair next to the bed.

'I said I wasn't going to be looked at by a sheila,' Mark wailed and Penny heard Derek smother a laugh. She took a step backwards and not so innocently stood on Derek's foot. That stopped his laughing.

'Mr Shields. I understand you've had another go-karting accident. Could you tell me exactly what happened?' Penny's voice was calm as she went to read his chart.

'I've already told a hundred or so people. Why don't you read about it because I'm sure *Woman's Day* would have been told, thanks to all of the nosy people around here.' He turned to face his friend. 'I told you I shouldn't have come back.' All he received was a grin back from Steve.

'Well, Mr Shields. You can either go through the rigmarole of answering my questions and letting me examine you—in which case I'll be out of here in ten minutes—or you can waffle on and make a general fuss while I question and examine you, in which case I'll be out of here in an hour or so. Which would you prefer?'

Penny didn't receive an answer. Not unless you could call a grunt an answer. She was sure that had Mark been able to cross his arms defensively he would have done so.

'I'll go and check on the X-rays,' Derek said and slipped away as a nurse came in and Penny began her examination.

True to her word, ten minutes later she had finished with Mark Shields and was in the registrar's office, conferring with Derek about Mark's X-rays. It was a cut and dried case of a comminuted humeral neck fracture that would need open reduction and internal fixation.

'How's James Anderson doing?' Penny asked and Derek smiled.

'As well as can be expected. No complications through the night, which is a good sign. Isn't Mr Wilson due to be transferred to the rehab hospital this week?'

'Yes.' Penny automatically collected the coffee-cups and took them to the sink. 'I'll stop in and see him. He could probably go tomorrow.'

'Who could go where?' Sam appeared in the doorway all neatly shaven and looking very refreshed.

'Barry Wilson. He could probably be transferred to the rehab hospital tomorrow. What do you think?' Penny knew that her voice sounded stilted.

'Sounds fine. Do you want to review him together after the theatre list?'

'Sure.' Penny was conscious of Derek listening intently to their conversation. He was seated in the middle of the room with Sam at the door and Penny still at the sink. Derek was looking from one to the other as though he was watching a tennis match.

They were all quiet for a moment, the silence growing unbearable, when Sam pointed to the X-rays on the viewing box.

'Are those Mark Shields's?' He came further into the room and had a look. 'You were right, Chalmers. Straightforward open reduction and internal fixation.'

'Thank you.' Derek was chuffed with the praise and stuck his tongue out at Penny.

Penny went over to the viewing box and took the X-rays down, placing them back into their packet. 'Well, I'd better go and get ready for Theatre.' She took the X-rays and fled the room.

Once inside the female changing-rooms, Penny sat down on a bench and hung her head. What was wrong with her? She put it down to Derek's teasing, especially when nothing had yet been worked out between herself and Sam.

Taking a deep breath, Penny pulled herself together and changed into her theatre blues. It would be a short list with Mark Shields and three other patients who required removal of the screws or plates that had fixed their fractures.

They completed the list with no complications and after she and Sam had assessed Barry Wilson, deciding that he could be transferred the following day, Penny fled the hospital, arriving home just after six o'clock. She knew that she was avoiding Sam and the inevitable discussion they were due to have but she needed the space.

She yawned while she flicked through her mail and ignored her answering machine's furiously flashing light. Even though she had slept for a good ten hours the night before Penny was still exhausted. She boiled an egg and had some bread for her dinner before going to bed.

An hour later she was still tossing and turning, unable to get comfortable. Untangling herself from the sheet, she tried again to settle down.

'This is ridiculous,' she said to the artificially dark-ened room. She reached her arm across the bed and grabbed another pillow. Placing it over her head, she sighed, hoping that the added darkness of the pillow would trigger the 'off' switch to her brain.

She breathed in deeply, willing her body to relax, and immediately knew the problem. The pillow smelled of Sam and Penny knew that after only one night of him holding her closely whilst she slept she was ruined for sleep hereafter.

She pulled the pillow from her head and embraced it tightly. What had Samuel Chadwick done to her? Not only was she doomed to forgo sleep but if she finally did drift off she'd dream about him, her body and mind begging for him.

Around nine o'clock Penny drifted off to sleep and when she awoke she found that she was still hugging the pillow tightly, still breathing in his scent. She rolled over and looked at the clock. Six-thirty. Penny realised that she'd forgotten to set the alarm again and was thankful that her body clock had woken automatically.

'Look what you've done to me, Sam,' she accused him out loud while she showered. 'I can't sleep and when I do I dream of you. I can't concentrate properly at work. I don't eat properly because I'm so busy trying to do anything and everything I can to get you out of my system. Studying, working, concentrating and ignoring you make me extremely tired and when I try to sleep I can't! It's a catch-22 situation.'

She shut the taps off with unnecessary force and continued with her morning routine. Griping to the air about the effect Sam was having on her life wasn't going to get her anywhere.

'He did what?' Penny exploded after Derek had quickly cornered her and dragged her into the registrar's office.

'He gave one of the nurses on the ward a marijuana cookie,' Derek said.

'I'll kill him. The man is an idiot. Is the nurse all right?' Penny continued to pace back and forth, running her fingers through her curls.

'She had heart palpitations and one of the other nurses took her to Casualty immediately. The last report I heard was that she was fine.'

'I'll kill him,' Penny kept muttering. 'Is she going to press charges?'

'I don't know. Penny, I think you ought to calm down because. . .'

'Calm down? Calm down? Mark Shields, through his own stupidity and selfishness, gave one of the nurses a marijuana cookie just to see what her reaction would be and you tell me to calm down? I don't think so, Derek.'

'Well, lower your voice at least,' Derek pleaded.

'I'll have to report it to Prof. I assume he doesn't know yet?'

'Not as far as I know.'

'Where's Mark Shields?'

'His friend Steve took him out in a wheelchair for some fresh air.' Derek stood up. 'Do you want me to come with you to tell Prof?'

'No. I'll do it.' Penny reached for the phone and dialled Sam's secretary. She replaced the receiver a few seconds later. 'He's not in yet. She'll page me when he arrives. I'd better go and check on the nurse.'

Penny went to Casualty and was directed to a cubicle where the orthopaedic nurse was lying down.

'Hi, Rebekah. Feeling better?' Penny slipped through the opening in the curtain and went to the bedside. Rebekah was a delicate woman with fine blonde hair pulled back into a bun and wide blue eyes. She was timid and shy, although extremely pretty.

'Yes, although I do feel rather foolish.' Rebekah

tried to sit up but Penny put a hand on her shoulder.

'Just rest. Why do *you* feel foolish?'

'I can't believe I ate it. I should never have taken it.'

'Rubbish. You weren't to know what it was and *he* should never have offered it. You know it's quite common when patients receive goodies that they share them with the staff and other patients. I'm just thankful that he didn't offer them around to the other patients. Don't you dare berate yourself for accepting that biscuit.'

'Thanks, Penny,' Rebekah smiled weakly. 'What happens now?'

'Do you want to press charges?'

'I don't know. I don't want to cause any problems.'

'Rebekah, if you don't press charges you may be letting Mark Shields know that he can get away with this and therefore do *more* damage. What happens when he sells these cookies to schoolchildren?'

'You're right. I just don't like making waves. What if he sends a gang out to get me or something like that?'

'I don't think he'd do that, despite how scary he looks with his tattoos. He's just an immature kid who thought he'd have a bit of fun at your expense. If your body had responded to the drug in the normal fashion you could have made serious errors in your work. Just imagine administering the wrong amount of antibiotics or not changing a dressing properly. The possibilities are endless, not to mention dangerous. We should be thankful that your body responded as it did.' Penny read her chart before replacing it at the end of the bed.

'You're right, Penny. I'll press charges. How do I go about it? Does Professor Chadwick need to know?' Rebekah's voice was wavering and Penny thought that it was all too much for her.

'Leave everything to me. I'll contact the police and

explain the situation to Prof. You try and relax. I'll come back and see you later.'

Penny hurried back to the registrar's office and made the necessary call to the police. They wouldn't be able to come until later that afternoon but that would give Penny time to speak with Sam.

It was an hour later when she finally received the page from his secretary and she made her way to his office. Where had he been all morning? Immediately the thought entered her head she banished it. What right did she have to know how Sam spent his private time? He was her boss and nothing more.

But you love him, a small voice inside her heart whispered, and Penny once again knew that from somewhere she'd have to find the courage to fight for him. She needed him, longed for him. Maybe they could have that chat now?

She lifted her hand to knock on the door but the wood vanished from beneath her knuckles as Sam stood in the entrance-way. All of her courage drained out of her body and she almost looked down, expecting to see it on the floor.

'Come in.' He stood back to let her enter. 'What's the problem this time? Or isn't there one?' He walked over to his desk and sat down, indicating for her to do the same.

'Unfortunately there is a problem,' and she quickly explained the situation. 'I've contacted the police but they won't get here until later this afternoon. When you go down to see Rebekah could you just reiterate that pressing charges is the right thing to do? She seemed very uncertain and I don't want her to change her mind.'

'Have you spoken to Mark Shields?'

'No. His friend, Steve, has taken him out into the

hospital grounds in a wheelchair. He seems like a decent chap and will hopefully talk some sense into Mark.'

'I think I'd better talk with Mr Shields. I know what your temper is like when you get a bee in your bonnet. I don't want him to press charges against *you*.'

Penny smiled at his comment. 'Know me that well, do you? You're right, of course. When Derek told me what had happened I was threatening to kill the man. Not that I ever would, mind you. It was just a figure of speech.'

'Speaking of speeches, when are you and I going to have our talk? Don't think I've forgotten about it because I haven't. I've just been letting you avoid me for the past day or so because I figured you needed more time.'

Penny was silent, unsure of what to say.

'See how well I know you.' His voice was as soft as a caress and Penny gasped at the look on his face. It was one of sheer splendour, or could it be. . .love? No! Sam couldn't possibly be in love with her? Could he?

CHAPTER TWELVE

'WHAT did Sam say?' Derek asked as he caught up with Penny a few minutes after she'd escaped from Sam's office.

'He said he'd talk to Mark Shields. Happy now?' Penny asked. 'Casualty is going to let us know when the police arrive to interview Rebekah and to take a statement from her.'

'Good. She's quite a shy person, isn't she?' Derek pondered.

'Fancy her, do you?' Penny teased.

'Well, you have to admit that she is a very attractive woman and if she's a timid, gentle person. . .' he paused and glared at Penny '. . .nothing at all like you, then she'd need someone to take care of her. To nurture her and. . .'

'Oh, stop,' Penny laughed. 'I'm going to be sick if you continue. You're hopeless, Derek. See a pretty face and you can't help yourself. Who do you think you are—a knight in shining armour?'

'Just call me Sir Galahad,' Derek joked before Penny's beeper sounded.

'Hopefully that's to tell me the police are here.' She made the brief call and nodded to Derek. 'Come on, Sir Galahad.' She grabbed his tie and pulled him along behind her. 'Saddle up your horse and go rescue the fair maiden.'

On their way to the cardio ward, which was where Rebekah had been taken, they passed Steve pushing a subdued-looking Mark Shields in the wheelchair

toward the ward. Penny tensed and ignored them completely. She was thankful that Sam was going to do the
chastising.

'Whew. Boy, am I glad that's over,' Penny said an
hour later as she, Derek and Sam left Rebekah's room.
'And you—' she placed her arm around Derek's shoulders '—were very supportive toward our colleague.'
She glanced over at Sam and smiled, her brown eyes
twinkling with mischief.

'Although I think she's going to need a lot of fol-
low-up support.' Sam joined in the teasing and Penny
laughed at the startled glance Derek gave his boss.

'Have you asked her out to dinner yet? You could
always ring Cindy-Lou and ask her to recommend
another restaurant,' Penny laughed and received a play-
ful punch from Derek.

'Cut it out, Hatfield. If there was another corridor to
walk down I'd do it, just to escape from the two of
you.' Derek tried to sound stern but he soon gave in
and joined their laughter.

When they reached the ward Penny looked at her
watch. 'I'd better go and say goodbye to Barry Wilson.
He's due to be transferred at four and it's almost
that now.'

'I'll join you,' Sam said, and the two of them entered
Mr Wilson's private room.

'Good to see you both.' Barry Wilson smiled at them
from his bed. 'I was hoping you'd both stop by.'

'We couldn't let you go without saying farewell,
even though Dr Hatfield will be seeing you in a few
days' time when she does her rounds at the rehabilitation hospital,' Sam explained as he reached for Mr
Wilson's chart.

'Where's Mrs Wilson?' Penny asked and before he
could answer the door opened again. Mrs Wilson

entered the room, holding a big bunch of flowers.

'Just the person,' she exclaimed and handed the flowers to Penny. 'It's a little thank you from both of us for the wonderful care and attention you've given over the past weeks.'

Penny was speechless and could feel the tears filling her eyes. 'Thank you,' she murmured at last.

'Now I hope the two of you have sorted things out and that we'll receive an invitation to the wedding,' Mrs Wilson continued.

Penny blushed and buried her nose in the flowers.

'Margaret,' her husband scolded, 'how many times have I told you not to be so forthright with your comments? Think about things, woman, before you say them. Can't you see you've embarrassed the young lass?'

'Oh, she'll be all right, won't she, Sam?' Mrs Wilson bent down to gather her knitting and placed it with Mr Wilson's belongings, ready for the move.

'She'll be fine, Margaret.' Sam placed an arm around Penny's shoulders and smiled down at her. Penny could feel herself beginning to perspire under the intensity in the room. She needed to escape. Things were happening too fast. Mrs Wilson was planning their wedding when they hadn't even talked. Especially when there was already another Mrs Chadwick on the scene somewhere.

'I'd better go and put these in some water,' Penny mumbled before she leaned forward and kissed Barry on the cheek. 'Thank you both. The flowers are beautiful and I promise I'll see you on Sunday at the rehab hospital.'

Her speech made, she left as fast as possible. She needed to go home to find some peace and solitude. Sam had let her flee again but she knew that her time was running out. She found Derek and told him she was leaving before rushing out to her resurrected car.

The drive home took longer than usual because of the peak-hour traffic. Many people were leaving work early because of the four-day break over Easter.

'Oh, no,' she said as she pulled the car into her driveway. 'The Easter dance is on Saturday and I have to buy shoes and a bag and everything else to match that dress.' She was angry with herself for forgetting and knew that she'd have to fight through the crowds tonight and go shopping.

She'd forgotten because doctors didn't usually get public holidays. They were on call twenty-four hours a day, seven days a week, twelve months a year. She plugged in the kettle and decided that it was time to pay her dues to her answering machine and listen to the messages from the past few days.

There were four from her parents and she switched the machine off and called them straight away. She made plans to visit them on Saturday and declined her mother's dinner invitation, telling her about the Easter dance that Derek was forcing her to go to.

When she'd hung up and made herself a cup of coffee, Penny listened to the rest of the messages. Janey had left several, begging Penny to call her.

'Penny, I desperately need to talk to you,' her best friend's voice pleaded. 'If you refuse to return my calls for much longer I'll send the police around to check that you are still alive.' Beep! The message ended.

'Penny. It's Janey again. It's Thursday morning and I know you're at work and that this call will cost me a fortune because it's not during the cheap times but I have a theory and wanted to run it past you.' Janey was speaking so fast that Penny had a bit of trouble understanding her.

'I know the reason why you're so mad at Sam and why you don't want anything to do with him. Craig has just dropped the bombshell that Sam was married.

'Let me just warn you that if you're not sitting down, I suggest you do so. Sam is no longer married. His wife died fourteen years ago, giving birth to their premature baby girl.

'His wife's name was Mary and she and Sam started going out during medical school. Near the end of their final year Mary accidentally became pregnant and so they married. They both managed to graduate and when Mary was only five and a half months pregnant she went into labour. Both she and the baby died.

'Please, please don't be mad at me for interfering in your lives. Craig tried to stop me but I love you both so much and knew from the moment I saw you together that you were made for each other.

'Don't give up your chance for happiness, Penny. Go to him. Tell him you love him. I think you'll be pleasantly surprised at his reaction.' Beep! The message ended. Ridiculously enough, the first thought that passed through Penny's mind was that Janey's message hadn't run out of tape on her machine.

Sam *wasn't* married. The thought reverberated around her head continuously. She sat there, unable to decide what to do first. Should she call him? Should she see him? She felt so foolish. How would he react when she told him how easily she had jumped to conclusions?

Penny wasn't sure how long she sat there, holding her cup of now very cold coffee. She felt as though she had betrayed Sam. Why hadn't she trusted him or confronted him?

A frown creased her brow as she remembered that evening Derek had taken her out to dinner. Who was the blonde lady he had been dining with? She had assumed that it was his wife but now she didn't know what to think.

'Tomorrow is another day,' she said to the darkened room. It was a saying her mother had used often during Penny's years of growing up. Another saying of her mother's popped into her head—Love holds all of the answers—and she finally knew that to be true.

She stood and returned her cup to the kitchen, tipping the cold liquid down the drain. Bed was next on the agenda, with all thoughts of shopping wiped from her mind. The talk that she had been postponing with Sam was now long overdue.

'What now?' Penny demanded of the inanimate pager as it beeped again. Forgetting that it was a public holiday and that Sam's secretary wouldn't be at work, Penny had been unable to make an appointment with him.

Instead she had managed to get his home phone number from Switchboard. They had arranged to meet at nine-thirty in his office and it was now twenty-seven minutes past nine. In the space of the last ten minutes her pager had sounded twice. This was the third time.

She looked at the number and rang through to Casualty.

'Dr Hatfield, can you come down, please?' the triage sister asked. 'A Mrs Maureen Brooker is being admitted and has specifically asked for you. She's in a bad way,' the sister added in a more subdued voice and Penny knew that her talk with Sam would yet again be put on the back burner.

'I'll be right there.' Penny took her white coat off the hook where it hung on hot March days like these and, after closing the door to the registrar's office, she hurried to Casualty.

'Dr Hatfield?' A tall burly policeman came across to Penny when she entered Maureen's cubicle. At Penny's nod he held the curtain aside and motioned for Penny to step back into the corridor. 'I'm Sergeant Haversham. We received a distress call an hour ago from Mrs Brooker's neighbour, reporting screams coming from the residence next door. On arrival we found her unconscious and in very bad shape, the husband still beating her with the leg of a broken coffee-table. The front door had been smashed in and various windows broken. Needless to say, the place was a mess.

'When we booked him we also discovered the restraining order Mrs Brooker had taken out on her husband. He's going nowhere for at least the next ten to fifteen years.'

Penny let out the breath she had been holding and slowly unclenched her fingers from the fists they had balled into.

'Thank you, Sergeant. If you wouldn't mind contacting me later today, I'll be able to fill out any necessary paperwork regarding Mrs Brooker's injuries. Right now, I'd like to give her a thorough examination and, if necessary, prepare her for theatre. Just call the hospital switchboard and have me paged.'

'Will do, Dr Hatfield.' Again he held the curtain open for her to enter, before motioning to his partner who had stayed in with Maureen while they had been talking.

'Hey,' Penny soothed as Maureen broke down into tears once the police officers had left. 'You're going to be fine. Don't you worry about a thing.' Penny looked over the blood-splattered clothes and the badly bruised face, hoping that it looked worse than it actually was.

Behind them the curtain swished as a sister entered, ready to assist Penny in her examination.

'Carol?' Maureen asked weakly.

'I'll have her called immediately,' Penny said and nodded to the sister who directly left to organise things. On the sister's return Penny began the examination, ordering removal of the plaster casts that were on Maureen's right arm and leg and requesting that they be X-rayed as well as her clavicle, ribs and skull.

They attended to the cuts, suturing one above the eye, one on the cheek and another across the palm of her left hand. Before she was taken to Radiology Penny examined the plaster on Maureen's right arm more thoroughly. She noticed that the plaster had been cracked and asked Maureen if she remembered how this had happened.

'I only remember that after he pushed me to the ground I saw him raise that piece of wood over his head, an evil glint in his eye, and I instinctively knew he was going to aim for my head. I closed my eyes and waited and the next thing I knew I was in an ambulance.'

She spoke quietly, her eyes closed. The orderly arrived to take her to Radiology and Penny made her way to Sam's office. She knocked and entered to find him on the telephone. He motioned for her to take a seat and from the sounds of his conversation he was almost finished.

'You took your time getting here.' His voice was light but his eyes spoke of his impatience.

'I had an emergency. Maureen Brooker's been readmitted. Her husband's bashed her again, even though there was a restraining order out on him.'

Penny stood and began to pace the floor.

'From what I can tell she shielded her head with her plastered arm. She doesn't remember doing it and I'm sure it was an instinctive reaction. He cracked the plaster so the force must have been incredible. He would have cracked her skull wide open and killed her instantly with that blow.'

'Who brought her in?' Sam asked, leaning back in his chair.

'The police. A neighbour alerted them after hearing screams coming from Maureen's house. When they arrived she was unconscious and he was still beating her. I just can't believe people actually do these things.' Penny shook her head in disgust and Sam stood and came to her side.

He reached for her hands and held them tightly. 'Neither can I. Is she in Radiology?'

Penny nodded as Sam led her back to the seat. 'The police will be contacting me later today to discuss her injuries further. They say her husband will get at least ten to fifteen years.'

'Why don't I make us some coffee and you can take a break while you're waiting for Mrs Brooker to return from Radiology?' Not waiting for an answer, he left the office. When he returned a few minutes later, carrying two cups of coffee, he asked, 'Are you going to the dance tomorrow night?' His question took her completely by surprise.

'Yes. Derek's forcing me to go and, considering he's already bought the tickets, I can't very well let him down.'

'Unless he's decided to escort Rebekah instead,' Sam said with a smile.

'I'd forgotten all about her. Have you heard how she's doing?'

'Fine.' He walked to the window, his back to her, and Penny took the opportunity to study him. He'd definitely lost weight in the past few weeks and she'd noticed that his eyes were looking a bit hollow. Hadn't he been sleeping either?

'Sam.' She knew her voice was husky and was happy when he turned and she saw the desire flare in his eyes at the way she said his name. 'I. . .'

'No, don't. We can't talk now,' he interrupted. 'I know we have to but please, Pen, not now.'

His words troubled her and she frowned as they sipped their coffee. Had he had second thoughts? Was he going to tell her who the blonde lady was? Was she someone special?

'I can tell your mind is working nineteen to the dozen and you can forget everything that it's wondering. We'll talk and sort things out but not right at this particular moment.'

As if to illustrate what he meant, Penny's pager sounded and she read the number of the radiology unit.

'Maureen Brooker must be finished,' she said and reached for his phone. 'Do you want to examine her? I'll most likely take her to Theatre straight away.'

'I have to give a lecture for the consultant orthopaedic conference this afternoon so I'm afraid I can't.' He drained his coffee and walked her to the door. Penny thought for one heart-stopping moment that he was going to kiss her but he pulled back at the last minute before pushing her gently out of the door.

It turned out that Maureen Brooker had a fractured clavicle, a Colles' fracture to her left wrist and had fractured three ribs on the right side and two on the left. Her previous fractures to the right arm and leg were both fine and were placed in splints. Her skull was intact thanks to the thick plaster of Paris cast that had been on her arm.

Theatre didn't take long and Penny set the Colles' fracture and strapped the ribs and clavicle. Ten minutes after she'd finished her pager beeped for what seemed like the hundredth time that day and Penny's involvement with the police department began.

When she finally arrived home she rang Janey's number, wanting to thank her friend for interfering, but no one was home. She went to her room and took out the black evening dress she was supposed to wear tomorrow night. She had no shoes that matched and wasn't sure what jewellery she should wear.

The phone rang, making her jump, and she snatched it up.

'Hi, Sis.' Eric's voice came across the line.

'Hi yourself,' Penny answered automatically.

'When are you coming down, Penny?' Eric asked enthusiastically.

'Why?' She knew her brother of old and cautiousness was definitely called for.

'Nothing bad. I've bought a car.'

'Great. So you want to show it off?'

'Let me take you for a spin, Sis. When do you get here?'

'Tomorrow.'

'What *time* tomorrow?' he asked impatiently.

'I don't know, Eric. Whatever time I get there.' Penny smiled into the receiver. 'Probably around ten, maybe eleven. It all depends what time I wake up,' she teased.

'Come earlier if you can. I'm so excited and I just can't wait to show you.'

'I promise to set my alarm and that's all I can do. If I ignore it or oversleep I'll be there when I get there.'

Penny tried not to laugh at his sigh of impatience.

'OK. See you tomorrow.'

'Hey. Aren't you going to tell me what kind it is or where you bought it or even what colour it is?' Penny asked, deciding not to tease him any more.

'I thought you'd never ask.' Eric took a breath and launched into details and Penny sat and dutifully listened to her brother. It was almost an hour later when she replaced the receiver in its cradle and went to bed.

Saturday morning was bright and Penny woke at eight and showered and dressed before packing her Easter eggs and heading off toward her parents' property. The day flew by as Eric showed her every inch of the car and took her for a leisurely drive to Victor Harbour after a scrumptious lunch.

She'd confided her dilemma about shoes and jewellery to her mother and had been promptly whisked off to the bedroom where she'd tried on various shoes and pieces of jewellery.

'This is the necklace I wore when your father proposed to me,' Ellen said as she clasped the delicate string of pearls around Penny's neck. 'Oh, darling. They look lovely on you.'

'They do, don't they?' Penny turned her head from side to side, admiring the tiny pearls that had taken many oysters years to make. 'May I borrow them?' Penny turned to face her mother.

'Certainly, dear.' Her mother's eyes misted over with tears as she looked at her daughter. 'You're in love, aren't you.' It was a statement, not a question and Penny nodded.

Did her lipstick need retouching? Was the dress too daring? Derek had told her he'd be late picking her up and as it was just after nine o'clock he'd be here any minute. She did a twirl and checked herself once again. The doorbell pealed and she sternly told her reflection that it was too late for any last-minute changes.

'I'm coming, Derek,' she told the door when the bell rang again. She opened the door but this time it wasn't Derek. It was Sam.

Penny stood in the doorway, mouth gaping open as her eyes hungrily drank in the sight of Sam in a tuxedo, one arm tucked behind his back.

As though he were pulling a rabbit from a hat, he swung his arm around, revealing an enormous bunch of gerberas of all colours, and held them out to Penny.

'For you,' he said softly and she reached out a shaking hand to grasp them. She stood back to let him enter and forced herself to go through the motions of putting the flowers into several vases.

'Where's Derek?' Penny asked but Sam silenced her with one finger across her lips and she began to tremble.

'No questions. Not yet. Get your bag and wrap, if you've got one, and we'll go.'

She did as he asked and within minutes she was seated in the Jaguar, heading toward the city.

'We're not going to the dance,' he announced and held up one hand for silence. 'I suggested to Derek that he take Rebekah to the dance instead of you.' Sam paused as he turned a corner. 'He seemed very pleased when I told him that I would be. . .*entertaining* you this evening.' He continued to drive and Penny soon recognised the route as they turned into his street.

He brought the car to a stop outside the house and Penny wondered why he didn't drive into the driveway. Too late to ask questions, she thought, as he was already out of the car and coming around to open her door.

'This way.' He placed one hand under her elbow and led her up to the door. She was grateful that his arm was so firm as it was pitch-black. Idly she wondered why the sensor light didn't come on when they reached the front porch. Sam opened the door but still didn't switch on any lights.

He led her up the stairs and, like a lamb to the slaughter, Penny followed. They walked down a short passageway and into a room. She could see the outline of a big bed and wondered if this was his room. He walked her over to an open window and relieved her of her bag before placing the briefest of kisses on her lips.

'Don't move from this spot,' he ordered before shutting the door as he disappeared from the room.

Penny was now thoroughly confused but stood rooted to the spot, unable to move even if she'd wanted to.

Suddenly the ground before her was illuminated. She saw a whole flock of wooden pink flamingoes scattered around his front yard, with a large signboard in the middle.

'PENNY, WILL YOU MARRY ME?' the sign read in big, bold letters. Penny was sure her heart skipped a beat when Sam walked onto the grass, went down on one knee and held one single, solitary red rose up to the window.

Penny's heart was singing, yes, yes, yes, as her feet took flight. She wrenched open the door and ran down the now brightly lit staircase, out the front door and into Sam's waiting arms. His body melded with hers as he kissed her passionately.

'We'd better go inside,' he whispered in her ear, and, taking her hand, he led Penny into the living room. As he flicked the switch the room was illuminated and Penny was treated to another surprise. A room full of gerberas.

'I see you've done your homework, Professor.'

Penny smiled as he seated her on the couch.

'Now is the correct time for any questions you might have, but first I'd like an answer to my question.'

'How can you think there would be any answer other than yes? I love you, Sam.' Funny, the words weren't as hard to say as she'd thought they'd be.

'Why did you withdraw, Penny? What happened?' His voice was earnest and she could read the pain in his eyes.

She took a deep breath and began. 'I'd been looking through some old medical school year-books with my father and found a photograph of you in your graduating year. You and your wife.'

'I thought it had to be something like that. Let me tell you whole story as there are many rumours still floating around. Mary and I had met in the last year of high school and were just good friends. When we started medical school together we naturally hung around together. We started to become more serious and before we knew what had happened Mary was pregnant. It was a shock to us both.

'Mary didn't know what to do so we were married as soon as possible. Three months later she went into premature labour. She shouldn't have died, Pen.' The sadness in his voice almost brought Penny to tears. She hated to see him hurting and she placed a comforting arm around his shoulders.

'They both died from haemolytic disease. Mary was Rh negative and the baby was positive. The doctor she was under performed an emergency Caesarean when there was no need to. They didn't test to see if any foetal cells had entered Mary's blood so she wasn't given any anti-D immunoglobulin. By the time they'd realised what had happened it was too late.

'I wasn't there for the birth. They wouldn't let me

in. I watched her die, knowing there was nothing I could do.' He looked at Penny, tears in his eyes. 'I held our daughter, though. I went down to the morgue and held our baby. I needed to.'

'Oh, Sam.' Penny kissed him lightly, sharing his pain.

'That doctor was negligent and I should have pressed charges but I didn't. I left that hospital, vowing I'd never return. From that day onward I demanded perfection of myself and, later on, of all my staff. I know I have a bad reputation for yelling at people but I will not tolerate incompetence, especially when someone's life is at risk.

'I also steered clear of any romantic involvements. I was quite happy to date women but there was no way in the world I was going to set myself up for another relationship when there was the possibility of failure.'

He paused for a moment and looked at Penny. 'Until I met you. At first I simply wanted you but I wasn't prepared for commitment. The more I got to know you, though, the more I needed to share your laughter, your intelligence, your beauty and your love.

'The morning after I arrived at Craig's and Janey's and you were in the kitchen making coffee, I knew that it was more than just a physical relationship I wanted from you. I was in uncharted grounds and didn't know which way was up.'

'You don't need to tell me,' Penny interrupted. 'I felt exactly the same way.'

'I was even jealous of Derek. That evening when I looked across the restaurant to find you laughing at something he'd said, I snapped. It was stupid to come over and say hello but I couldn't help myself. I was eaten up with jealousy, even though you'd already told me you were just friends.' He reached out and smoothed a lock of hair off her forehead.

Penny cleared her throat, knowing that she had to ask the question. 'Who was that woman you were with that night?'

'My cousin, Kathryn. She was in Adelaide for one night on a business trip from Sydney. We don't see a lot of each other but when we're in the same state we look each other up.'

'I thought she was your wife.' Penny's voice was quiet and she realised that she was trembling.

'I can understand that. Why didn't you confront me? If you thought I was a married man playing around why did you just stop everything cold? Why not have it out?'

'I was too much in love with you. It wasn't until Derek, Janey and even the Wilsons told me to fight for you that I realised there could be a rational explanation. I thought long and hard and decided they were right. I was going to talk to you a few days ago but we've just had one emergency after another.'

'Tell me about it,' he joked and they laughed, easing the tension in the air.

'I'd already decided to confront you when Janey left a message on my answering machine, telling me about your wife and that she'd died. I couldn't believe my ears.'

'Oh, Pen, we've wasted so much time. . .' His words were cut short by someone leaning on the doorbell. Sam returned a few minutes later, laden with boxes of food.

'Chinese,' he said in answer to her unspoken question. Could he read her mind now?

'You've thought of everything, haven't you?' Penny laughed as he unpacked the food.

'Absolutely.'

'Gerberas, roses, flamingos and now Chinese food.

You must have *really* pumped Janey for information.'

'I did. Although there is one surprise that I thought up all by myself. Come,' he said and held out a hand to her. Her led her to a door then told her to close her eyes before he led her the rest of the way.

'Open your eyes,' he commanded and she did.

They were in the kitchen and directly in front of her was a shining new dishwasher.

'Why?' she laughed and turned into his arms.

'Because I love you and because I can't have those surgeon's hands all chapped from doing dishes, can I?'

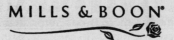

MILLS & BOON®

Medical Romance™

Books for enjoyment this month...

THE IDEAL CHOICE	Caroline Anderson
A SURGEON'S CARE	Lucy Clark
THE HEALING TOUCH	Rebecca Lang
MORE THAN SKIN-DEEP	Margaret O'Neill

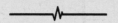

Treats in store!

Watch next month for these absorbing stories...

RESPONDING TO TREATMENT	Abigail Gordon
BRIDAL REMEDY	Marion Lennox
A WISH FOR CHRISTMAS	Josie Metcalfe
WINGS OF DUTY	Meredith Webber

SINGLE LETTER SWITCH

A year's supply of Mills & Boon Presents™ novels— absolutely FREE!

Would you like to win a year's supply of passionate compelling and provocative romances? Well, you can and the're free! Simply complete the grid below and send it to us by 31st May 1997. The first five correct entries picked after the closing date will win a year's supply of Mills & Boon Presents™ novels (six books every month—worth over £150). What could be easier?

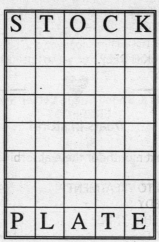

S	T	O	C	K
P	L	A	T	E

Clues:

A   To pile up

B   To ease off or a reduction

C   A dark colour

D   Empty or missing

E   A piece of wood

F   Common abbreviation for an aircraft

Please turn over for details of how to enter ☞

1

How to enter...

There are two five letter words provided in the grid overleaf. The first one being STOCK the other PLATE. All you have to do is write down the words that are missing by changing just one letter at a time to form a new word and eventually change the word STOCK into PLATE. You only have eight chances but we have supplied you with clues as to what each one is. Good Luck!

When you have completed the grid don't forget to fill in your name and address in the space provided below and pop this page into an envelope (you don't even need a stamp) and post it today. Hurry—competition ends 31st May 1997.

Mills & Boon® Single Letter Switch
FREEPOST
Croydon
Surrey
CR9 3WZ